"My daughter is on her way to you now. I need you to promise to keep her safe. Don't forget she's just a child." Cassidy turned toward the windows. "A child who should not have to make this choice."

"She will be with us for her Sunrise Ceremony."

"Are there drugs involved? Peyote or some such? Because I will bust you, all of you, so fast."

Clyne rolled his eyes. "You see. This is the trouble. You don't know anything about us."

"I know it's illegal to give drugs to a minor."

"We won't."

"Fine. Dress her up in feathers and beads. It won't change her." She stomped across the room and then back, her arms flapping occasionally. Finally she stopped before him. "I can't believe I kissed you."

He gave her a satisfied smile. "Well, you did."

NATIVE BORN

JENNA KERNAN

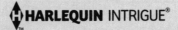

For Jim, always.

Recycling programs
for this product may
not exist in your area.

ISBN-13: 978-0-373-74967-6

Native Born

Copyright © 2016 by Jeannette H. Monaco

Printed in U.S.A.

™ www.Harlequin.com

Jenna Kernan has penned over two dozen novels and has received two RITA® Award nominations. Jenna is every bit as adventurous as her heroines. Her hobbies include recreational gold prospecting, scuba diving and gem hunting. Jenna grew up in the Catskills and currently lives in the Hudson Valley of New York state with her husband. Follow Jenna on Twitter, @jennakernan, on Facebook or at jennakernan.com.

Books by Jenna Kernan

Harlequin Intrigue

Apache Protectors

Shadow Wolf
Hunter Moon
Tribal Law
Native Born

Harlequin Historical

Gold Rush Groom
The Texas Ranger's Daughter
Wild West Christmas
A Family for the Rancher
Running Wolf

Harlequin Nocturne

Dream Stalker
Ghost Stalker
Soul Whisperer
Beauty's Beast
The Vampire's Wolf
The Shifter's Choice

Visit the Author Profile page at Harlequin.com for more titles.

CAST OF CHARACTERS

Clyne Cosen—As a tribal council member for the Black Mountain Apache tribe, Clyne is not going to let the FBI set up shop on their sacred land. His opposition brings him smack into conflict with an appealing FBI agent who happens to be the woman who adopted his baby sister.

Cassidy Walker—An FBI field agent and an outsider. Her drug trafficking investigation takes her onto tribal lands and right into conflict with Clyne Cosen, the man who is trying to overturn her child's adoption and has also managed to crack her carefully cultivated emotional control.

Amanda Walker—This twelve-year-old adopted daughter of Cassidy Walker has just discovered that she was born **Jovanna Cosen** and is a full member of the Black Mountain Apache tribe.

Donald Tully—Cassidy's supervisor with the FBI. It's his business to assist in the investigation, but his choices raise some serious questions.

Johnny and Lamar Parker—The brothers of the armed smuggler Cassidy shot and killed. Their appearance on the rez can't be a coincidence. Can it?

Griffin Lipmann—The representative of Obella Chemicals is here for damage control after a major chemical spill contaminates the Salt River. But how far is he willing to go to stop Clyne from rallying his people against his company?

Manny Escalanti—This gang leader is working with at least one Mexican cartel. Getting him to turn over his associates might be as hard as proving he's involved.

Luke Forrest—The Cosen brothers' uncle and half brother to their dad. He's a war hero turned FBI field agent.

Ronnie Hare—The parole officer and Apache from the Salt River tribe has gone MIA since it was discovered he was running messages from the cartels to the American distributors.

Gabe Cosen—The second oldest Cosen brother, Gabe is the chief of the Tribal Police on Black Mountain. But why would this Apache lawman allow the Feds to assist in his investigation?

Chapter One

If Cassidy Walker had known what would happen that Monday morning, she most certainly would not have worn her new suit. As an FBI field agent, Cassidy had drawn the short stick on assignments today or perhaps this was her boss's idea of humor. He knew there was no love lost between her and Tribal Councillor Clyne Cosen. Yet here she was watching his back.

Did her boss think it was funny assigning her to Cosen's protection or was this still payback for her bust in January? Was it her fault he was skiing in Vail when she and Luke had found both the precursor and the second meth lab? He'd gone back to the Organized Crime Drug Enforcement Task Force to report his agents had made the bust, but he hadn't been there.

Another feather in Cassidy's cap.

She glanced over at her supervisor, Donald Tully. Because of his dark glasses, she could not see his eyes. But his smirk was clear enough. The man could hold a grudge.

Cassidy adjusted her polarized lenses against the Arizona sun. From her place behind the speaker, she scanned her sector for any sign of threat. Her assignment was to protect the speaker from harm. This was not her usual duty, but today the stage was filled with a mix of state and national officials and that meant all hands on deck.

Outdoor venues were the most dangerous, but the Apache tribal leaders had insisted on staging the rally here in Tucson's downtown river park.

As the next speaker took the podium she tried hard to ignore his rich melodious voice and the fine figure he cut in that suit jacket. The long braid down his back had been dressed with leather cords and silver beads. His elegant brown hands rested casually on either side of the podium. He had no speech. Clyne Cosen, tribal councilman for the Black Mountain Apache, didn't need one.

She gritted her teeth as she forced her gaze to shift restlessly from one person to the next, looking for anyone lifting something other than a cell phone. Judging from the wide-eyed stares from most of the women in the crowd and the way they were using up their digital storage snapping photos of the handsome tribal leader, it seemed she was not the only one who admired the physical presence of this particular speaker.

Cassidy glanced at the cheery arrangement of sunflowers just before her feet and resisted the urge to kick them off the stage. She had a personal grudge with this speaker and was struggling to maintain her focus.

The next up would be Griffin Lipmann, the president of Obella Chemicals. The Bureau had already suited Lipmann in body armor as this latest spill had made him public enemy number one in the minds of many. He was the main reason the Bureau had lobbied to hold this rally indoors. Of course Clyne Cosen and his band of Apache activists wanted to be right beside the river that was now an unnatural shade of yellow.

Cosen knew the power of the television cameras and social media. Until he finished speaking, he was her damned assignment and the way he was going on and on, it didn't look like he'd be stopping anytime soon.

She tried to set aside her personal issues with him and do her job. But her teeth kept gnashing and her hands kept balling into fists. Soon she'd be meeting Clyne in a personal capacity, him and all his brothers. Damn that Indian Child Welfare Act. It had left her with no options, no more appeals. Nothing but the judge's final ruling. For the first time in her life she considered breaking the law and running for Mexico.

She glanced back to Clyne Cosen, who now motioned toward the ruined water. She knew he had spotted her before he took his place because his usually sure step had faltered and his generous smile had slipped. Did it make him nervous to have her behind him, watching his back? She hoped so.

Her gaze shifted again, from one face to the next. Watching the expressions, keeping track of their hands. The sunlight poured down on them. It was only a little past ten in the morning but the temperature was already climbing toward eighty. March in Arizona, her first one and hopefully her last. She'd planned to take the first assignment out of here, Washington hopefully or New York. She'd certainly earned a promotion after her last case. But now, if her daughter would be here she might… If they won, would she even be allowed to see her?

Cassidy jerked her attention back to her assignment. How she hated the outdoor venues. There were just an endless number of places to secure.

A woman wearing a cropped T-shirt reached into her purse. Cassidy leaned forward for a better look as Clyne lifted his voice, decrying the carelessness with which Obella Chemicals had released the toxic mix into their water. The woman lifted a silver cylinder from her bag and for one heart-stopping moment Cassidy thought it was the barrel of a gun. She reached under her blazer, gripping her pistol as the woman fumbled with a white cord. She plugged the cord into her cell phone and the other end into the cylinder. A charger, Cassidy realized and relaxed.

That was when the three-foot-tall vase of sunflowers beside the podium exploded.

"Shots!" she shouted, and took down her assignment, diving on Clyne's back as other agents moved before the line of dignitaries on the stage, making a human shield.

Griffin Lipmann, the representative from Obella Chemicals, hit the stage unassisted. His personal security force sprang before him an instant later, hustling him off the stage.

Her weight pitched Clyne forward, but he kept his balance, spinning toward her and then hitting the second flower arrangement before toppling backward onto the stage with her sprawled on top of him. She pushed off his torso and drew her weapon.

He tried to sit up.

She pressed a hand into his chest.

"Down!" she ordered, ignoring the firm body

beneath her as she lifted her weapon and rolled to a kneeling position.

Two more agents stepped before them. Below the stage the audience members screamed and many turned to run.

"What's happening?" Clyne asked.

She didn't know. It could have been a shooter or some kid with a slingshot.

"Up," she snapped. "That way."

Cassidy followed the plan, tugging Clyne up and guiding him off the back of the stage, pushing him before her. He was two steps down the staircase and she had reached the top step when something struck her in the back. It felt like someone hit her with a Louisville Slugger right below her left shoulder blade. The impact was so strong that it pitched her forward onto Clyne Cosen's back. He staggered. Then he grabbed both her forearms and kept running, making for the cover of the side entrance of the waterfront hotel. Cassidy tried and failed to draw a breath. The blow had knocked the wind right out of her and all she could manage was a wheezing sound.

He carried her along like a monkey on his back, never slowing as he stretched his long legs into a full-out run that made the wind whistle in her ears. Those Apache moccasins he wore were tearing up the ground faster than any cross trainers she'd ever owned. Local law enforcement held open the door. Cassidy glanced backward as they charged into the corridor.

The crowd erupted into chaos as men and women scrambled to clear the riverfront park that had turned into a shooting gallery. A bullet struck the building beside the exit and a chunk of concrete flew into the air. The officer holding the door moved to cover as Clyne grasped the closing door and hurtled inside.

Cassidy peered over his shoulder as the striped wallpaper and heavily painted desert scenes flashed past. She wanted to tell him to put her down or to make for the safe room. But she still hadn't succeeded in drawing a breath and now feared she was going to faint.

Finally he slowed, moving to the wall and swinging her around as if she were a dance partner instead of a rag doll. He made her feel small by comparison. Clyne Cosen had to be six-four in his flat footwear.

He lowered her to the ground in an alcove beside one of the restrooms. She slumped against the wall. Only then did she regain her breath. It came in a tortured gasp. Her eyes watered but she could see he'd gone pale.

Dignitaries and FBI agents rushed past them toward the rendezvous point. Cassidy still gripped her pistol.

"I think I'm hit," she said.

Clyne pulled off her blazer, sticking his finger through a hole in the back as he did so.

"Damn, that was Armani," she said.

"The shooter?" he asked.

She shook her head. Clearly Councillor Cosen did not know fashion. He dropped the blazer in her lap and she stroked the gray pinstripe like a sick cat. Then she holstered her weapon.

He expertly unclipped her shoulder holster and she grasped his wrist.

"Don't touch the gun," she said.

He met her scowl for scowl.

"Fine. You do it." He lifted his hands as if he was surrendering to her custody.

She did and the motion made her wince, but she managed to slip out of her holster and draw it down into her lap. When she finished she was trembling and sweat glistened on her skin.

Cosen tugged her blouse from the waistband of her slacks. A moment later she heard a rending sound as he tore her pristine white blouse straight down the center of her back. Then he leaned her forward to drag her blouse down off both shoulders so they puddled at her wrists. She now sat in only her slacks, practical shoes, body armor and her turquoise lace bra.

She flushed the color of ripe strawberries, a hazard of those with fair skin and felt her face heat as his eyebrows lifted. He hesitated only a moment and muttered something that sounded like "none of the guys in my unit wore lace."

She felt the pressure of his hand on her back.

"Perforation," he said, pressing on the sore place on her back. "Got you here."

She bit her lip to keep from whimpering. More people ran past in the corridor but she could see only trousers and dark shoes.

"Get me up," she said.

He ignored her, splaying a hand over her chest and pitching her forward like a ventriloquist's dummy. A moment later his other hand slipped under her vest at the back, rooting around.

"Vest is distorted right over your heart," he said. He released a long breath. "Didn't penetrate," he said. His hand stroked her back, skimming over her bra and out from beneath her vest. "No blood. Your vest caught it."

He eased her back until she leaned against the wall. He was propped on one knee as he looked down at her, his eyes were the color of polished mahogany.

"Still need a hospital," he said.

She flapped her arms, now decorated with what was left of her Ann Taylor white blouse. He'd torn the collar right off the back as if he were tearing tissue paper.

She tried for a full breath and didn't make it.

"Hurts like hell, doesn't it?" he asked.

It did.

How did he know that?

But then she remembered. Clyne Cosen was a former US marine. His jacket didn't mention that he had taken lead.

His smile held and she felt herself drawn in. Three words from his character profile bounced around in her head like a Ping-Pong ball dropped on concrete.

Charismatic.

Charming.

Persuasive.

"Took one here and here." He pointed to his stomach and ribs. Making them part of an elite club, she supposed. The two of them. Only she was the one struggling with her breathing.

"A vest saved my life once before."

She didn't understand. He hadn't been hit. She'd kept him from that, protecting him like she was in the secret service and he was the president.

"Before?" she asked.

He pressed his open palm over her middle, his fingers splayed over her abdomen and she swore she could feel his touch even through the body armor. He met her stare.

"Agent Walker, you just saved my life."

Chapter Two

"You can thank me later," Cassidy said. The bullet meant for Cosen had struck her in the back. She'd done her job, acted like a human shield and was trying very hard not to feel pissed about it.

Who wanted him dead? she wondered.

Cassidy slipped the shoulder harness over her right side and winced as she reached to get that left arm through. She managed it.

"Let me help," he said, reaching for the buckle.

"Did I warn you about the gun?"

He drew back. Once she had it clipped she was sweating like a marathon runner. But she still managed to drag her gray pinstripe blazer over her body armor, removing the view of turquoise lace from Clyne and any of the persons in the hallway. The tattered remains of her sleeves peeked out from the cuff of her ruined jacket.

She pushed off and he helped her up. Cassidy resisted the urge to bat his hand away.

"You're uninjured?" she asked.

"Yes. But you need to see a doctor."

"You carrying?" she asked, trying to surmise if he wore a holster under his blazer or clipped to the belt that sported an elaborate turquoise and red coral buckle. Her gaze dipped south of his buckle and she flushed. And wouldn't you know it, when she lifted her gaze it was to find Cosen's gaze intent and his body perfectly still. Only now the tension in his tightly coiled muscles seemed sexual and arousing as all get-out.

"Sorry," she said.

He made a sound in his throat that fell somewhere between a growl and an acknowledgment.

She shook her head to clear the unwelcome arousal that stole through her. "Rendezvous point. Come on. Not safe here." Man, it hurt to talk.

Cassidy motioned for him to proceed down the hall. They'd made it about halfway when two of the field agents from her unit, Pauling and Harvey, appeared in the hall. Pauling came first, jogging so the sides of his suit coat flapped open to reveal both the shield on his belt and the butt of his pistol under his left arm. Keith Pauling was young, hungry and a former army ranger, with neatly trimmed hair and a hard angular face that screamed Fed from a hundred yards. Behind him came Louis Harvey, more experienced, heavier set but the haircut was a dead ringer.

"She's been shot," said Clyne.

Harvey took charge of Clyne and Pauling flanked Cassidy as they ushered them to the rendezvous room and her supervisor, who no longer looked smug.

"Walker. What took you so long?" he asked.

"She's been shot," Clyne said again.

Cassidy cast him a look. She didn't need him as her mouthpiece. Her ribs were feeling better and she'd be damned if she was going to spend the afternoon in the hospital when they had a shooter out there.

Clyne was herded away. He gave her one last long look over his shoulder, his braid swinging as he went. He was one of the most handsome men she had ever met and for just a moment, the confident mask slipped and she saw her daughter's face. The resemblance took her breath away.

Amanda. The arch of the brow, the worry in those big brown eyes. And then he was gone.

She scowled after him. If she had saved his life, then he had also protected hers. When other speakers on stage had run or fallen or flattened to the platform, Clyne had acted like a soldier, recognized that she was injured and carried her to safety.

She hated to owe him anything and wondered if he felt the same. She had met him before this. On a snowy evening on the Black Mountain reservation while investigating a meth ring. And again in court when her attorneys succeeded in delaying the process for challenging her daughter's adoption.

Cassidy saw a medic first, who decided that her ribs were bruised. The slug that they dug from her vest appeared to be a thirty caliber. She declined transport and borrowed an FBI T-shirt from Pauling that was still miles too big for her. The navy blue T said FBI in bold yellow lettering across the front and back. She covered what she could with the blazer.

Her people had already found the location of the shooter, now long gone. He'd left at least one rifle cartridge behind, despite taking two shots.

"He was on the roof of the adjacent hotel," said Tully. Her new boss peered at her with striking blue eyes. His hairline had receded to the point that it was now only a pale fringe clipped short at the sides of his head, but his face was thin and angular with a strong jaw and eyes that reminded her of a bird of prey.

She knew from his previous comments that

he liked running their unit and didn't like that she wanted out. He took it as some kind of black mark that she was not satisfied to bake out in this godforsaken pile of sand called Arizona. But Cassidy wanted to join a team that chased the big fish, not the endless flow of traffickers and illegals that ebbed and flowed over the boarder like a tide.

Tully plopped her down before a computer and made her write her report. While the others moved out to investigate; she sat in the control room. The reporting didn't take long. After she finished, she went over the footage of the event with one of the techs, watching her movements when the vase exploded from the first blast and then the proceeding mayhem. They had not stationed on the roofs because the threat was not deemed great enough to warrant the added security. If they had, her people might have been in place when the shooter arrived.

Her partner returned. Luke Forrest was Black Mountain Apache and Clyne's uncle, though as she understood it, he was Clyne's father's half brother and born of a different father and clan, though she didn't understand the clan system very well. Luke had not applied to the Bureau, but had been recruited right out of the US marines.

"How you feeling?" he asked.

"Bored," she said.

He laughed, his generous smile coming easily on his broad mouth.

"Well, there's worse things," said Luke.

His hair was short, his frame was athletic and slim and he only vaguely resembled Clyne around the eyes and brows.

Cassidy stared at Luke and wondered what Clyne's mother had looked like because she was Amanda's biological mother, too.

"What?" said Luke.

"Did you know Clyne's mother?"

"Of course."

"What was she like?"

He gave her an odd look, but answered. "Beautiful. Strong. Protective of her kids."

Cassidy nodded. Strong and beautiful, just like Clyne, she realized.

Why was she comparing everyone to Clyne Cosen? With any luck she wouldn't have to see him again. Her stomach twisted, knowing from her attorney that she would lose. Clinging to the only loophole allowed in the Indian Child Welfare Act. Thank God her daughter had turned twelve last June. Of course neither had known her real birthday until recently and had always celebrated on her adoption day on February 19.

"Where've you been?" she asked.

His eyes did that thing, the quick narrowing before his face returned to a congenial expression.

"Luke?"

He chuckled. "I must be losing my edge. I was with Tully and with Gabe Cosen. They're both on the joint task force."

She knew that Gabe had been invited belatedly to the joint drug enforcement task force that had been behind the operation to find the mobile meth lab and precursor needed to make the drugs. They had done an end run around Gabe, the chief of the tribal police force, and her partner because they were both Black Mountain Apache and therefore also suspects. Reasonable precaution, she had thought at the time. Now she felt differently.

"Listen, I'm sorry they left you out of the loop," she said.

"Yeah. Me, too." He gave her a long look. "You sure you're okay? You had a close call today."

"Yeah." Cassidy waved away his concerns as if they were smoke.

She refused to think about it, refused to consider that her daughter might have been left without a mother, again. Would Amanda then be turned over to her birth family?

She focused on what Luke had said. "So

does Tully think this has to do with the bust on Black Mountain?"

"It might. Might be someone after Obella Chemicals. Hell, it might be someone *from* Obella Chemicals."

"In other words, they have no leads."

Forrest shook his head.

"Tully said that he thinks Clyne Cosen was the target. Gabe Cosen agrees and wants his brother to have added security detail when off the rez."

"Reasonable," said Cassidy.

Forrest rubbed his chin and Cassidy knew he was holding back.

"Spill it."

"Your name came up as a possibility, too." He gave an apologetic shrug.

Her first reaction was indignation but she reined that in. "They figure how I shot myself in the back?"

Forrest chuckled. "Yeah, that did put a chink in their theory."

"Anyway, we're trying to get Clyne to accept protection. He's resisting," said Forrest.

"You think Tully will pick you?" Luke Forrest would make sense. He spoke Apache, knew the culture and the tribe. He'd blend in while the other agents would stick out like flies on rice.

"Don't know. Doesn't matter if Clyne won't

take us up on the offer. Plus we're still on cleanup with the Raggar case."

Which was proving much easier now that Gabe Cosen was on board. They had the meth lab and the precursor and were working on shutting down the distribution ring, run by mob boss Cesaro Raggar, currently in federal prison. She knew this because she'd been pissed not to get that assignment herself, when she was the one who'd responded to Gabe Cosen's call for backup once the precursor had been located. "How's the youngest brother doing?"

"Kino?" Luke rubbed his neck reflexively in the place his youngest nephew had taken a bullet. "Healing. And back to work on the tribal force."

As a tribal police officer, she knew. He'd also been a Shadow Wolf working on the border, tracking smugglers with his brother Clay. The Shadow Wolves were an elite team of Native American trackers working under Immigration and Customs Enforcement to hunt and apprehend drug traffickers on the Arizona border.

"Anyway, Gabe mentioned to Tully about the petition to overturn."

Cassidy's gaze flashed to Forrest and held.

"You should have told him, Cassidy. He's talking about pulling you off the Raggar case."

Which was exactly why she had not told Tully
about the custody battle.

"That has nothing to do with me doing my
job. Damn it, Luke. I've been on this since the
beginning. I've put in the time and I deserve to
see it through." Plus she knew bringing down
Raggar and Manny Escalanti would give her
the commendation she needed to earn a promotion to a major field office. Escalanti was the
leader of the Black Mountain's only gang, the
Wolf Posse. He'd managed to insulate himself
on the reservation and by using others to run
his errands. Cassidy wanted him bad.

Forrest shrugged. "It's a problem."

Clyne burst back into the room with her boss
and his brother Gabe Cosen on his heels. Gabe
scanned the room, met her gaze and did a quick
clinical sweep before moving on. He kept his
gun hand clear and immediately stepped out of
the doorway to a position where he could see
anyone approach the entrance. She smiled in
admiration. The man would make a good agent,
she decided, thinking that being the chief of
police on the rez seemed a waste of his talents.

"Councilman Cosen, please," said Tully. "We
can't guarantee your safety."

"Your guarantee. We all know what a guarantee from the federal government is worth."

Man, she could see the chip on his shoulder

from clear across the room. If she had it right, his tribe was one of the few that had remained on their land because they had succeeded in making a deal with the federal government that had been kept.

"It would be easier with your consent," said Gabe. "We are only talking about the times when you come down off Black Mountain."

"I'd rather have you," said Clyne, his dark eyes flicking to his younger brother.

"Well, I already have a job on the rez. These folks are much better prepared to watch your back, as evidenced by Agent Walker here."

Clyne came up short when he spotted her.

Gabe's comment forced Clyne to look at her. Cassidy sucked in a breath and felt the twinge at her ribs. Why did the simple connection of his gaze and hers make her skin buzz with an electricity? Oh, this was really bad.

He looked away and Cassidy exhaled. Unfortunately her skin still tingled. It was his charisma. Had to be. Because she refused to consider that she was attracted to Clyne Cosen.

"It's bad enough that you've got DOJ and these agents swarming all over Black Mountain," said Clyne. She knew that he didn't like Department of Justice or FBI, really any federal agency, on Indian land. But his words lacked the authority of a moment before and his gaze slipped to meet hers again before bouncing away. He wiped his mouth. If she didn't know better she would say he was rattled.

"Yes, and one of them died taking that load of chemicals. And you didn't mind them using their helicopter to transport Kino to the hospital down here."

Cassidy had arrived on scene just after the shooting Gabe mentioned. Kino had been hit in the neck. He would have bled to death if not for the transport.

Clyne scowled and damn if she didn't find him even more appealing. Now Cassidy was scowling, too.

"I won't object to protection for gatherings off the rez," he said at last. "Are we done?"

It seemed Clyne was as anxious to be away from them as she was to see his back.

"Almost," said Gabe. "I want to request a new DOJ agent be appointed to the joint task force to replace the fallen agent, Matt Dryer."

"Easily done," said Tully.

"And," said Gabe glancing first to his brother and then to Cassidy. He held her gaze as he spoke. "I request that Luke Forrest and Cassidy Walker be assigned to Black Mountain to assist in our investigation and report back to the joint task force."

"No," said Clyne.

Gabe turned to his elder brother as the two faced off. Clyne was slightly taller. Gabe slightly broader.

"I am required to notify tribal council of the presence of federal authorities on the reservation. I am not required to obtain their permission. This is your notice."

Clyne's teeth locked and his jaw bulged. Cassidy had to force herself not to step back. If the man could summon thunder it would surely have been rumbling over his head.

"Perhaps an agent other than Walker?" suggested Tully.

Gabe shook his head, his gaze still locked on Clyne. "Her."

Cassidy swallowed. She didn't understand why Police Chief Cosen would make such a play when his brother was against it. Her boss looked leery as well, likely because he now knew of the custody battle boiling between them. But she wanted the assignment because she wanted to continue her investigation and there was only so much she could do from Phoenix when the main player, Manny Escalanti, never left his nest on Black Mountain.

But why would Gabe Cosen want her? It didn't make sense and she suspected a trap. Was he trying to gain some advantage in the adoption battle? If so, she couldn't see it.

Clyne now leaned toward Gabe with a hand on his hip, which was thankfully clear of any weapon. Gabe settled for folding his arms over his chest and smiling like a man who knew he had won this round. Cassidy didn't think it was over, because Clyne looked like a bull buffalo just before a charge.

Their uncle Luke Forrest stepped between them, placing a hand on the shoulder of each brother.

"It won't be so bad," he said to his nephew. "Just like I'm visiting. And I sure won't mind sitting at your grandmother's table a time or two."

Tully glanced at her with an open look of assessment. She thought he was trying to puzzle this out as well and had also come up empty.

"All right, then," said Tully and pointed at Cassidy. "Agents Walker and Forrest, you are reassigned to Black Mountain until further notice."

Clyne glared at her and her wide eyes narrowed to meet the challenge in his gaze.

"Yes, sir," she said.

Chapter Three

"But why would he choose me?" Cassidy asked.

"Damned if I know," said Tully. "Because you saved his brother's life?"

Her partner, Luke Forrest, spoke up. "Don't you see a conflict of interest here?"

"It's Chief Cosen's call," said Tully. "One thing I know about Agent Walker is that she does her job. She proved it again today."

She couldn't tell if he was proud of her or still annoyed. But it was true. If she wanted Clyne Cosen dead, that had been her chance.

"Yes, sir." It was automatic, her response. Inside her head she was shouting, *No!* But that was the voice of emotion. The one that she ignored whenever possible.

"Walker. Forrest. You are assigned to the Organized Crime Drug Enforcement Task Force."

"Yes, sir."

Cassidy groaned. She didn't need to be on

another committee. Especially one made up of state, local and federal authorities. What she needed was to be in the field. They'd been getting close to Ronnie Hare and that bust might be all she needed to gain her transfer.

"Since you are Apache, I expect you to be able to do some recon and find out if there is anything going on up there that would lead someone to take a shot at Tribal Councillor Cosen."

"Yes, sir," said Agent Forrest.

Her daughter. The basketball game that she'd promised she would attend.

"I need to make arrangements for my daughter."

"Go on, then."

Clyne's scowl deepened.

Cassidy moved to the far side of the room to make a call to her mother-in-law. After Cassidy's husband, Gerard, had been killed in action, Diane Walker had moved west to help her pick up the slack. Cassidy had no family of her own, and Gerard had been Diane's only child. She made the call, apologized and disconnected. It was not the first time she had been unexpectedly sent on an assignment. It was the first time that that assignment was challenging her custody in federal court.

Cassidy glanced back to the waiting three

men. She had one more important call to make to Amanda, the only thing more important than her job.

"Hi, pumpkin. You at school?"

"Mom, school ended hours ago. I'm at the rec center. The game. Remember? Where are you? Warm-up is almost over."

She glanced at her watch and saw it was nearly four in the afternoon.

"Right. You all warmed up?" she asked, turning her back on the men.

"Where are you?" asked Amanda.

"I'm still in Tucson." Her daughter groaned. "Grandma is on the way."

"Oh, Mom!"

"Listen. There was some trouble. You'll see it on the news."

"Mom?" Her daughter's voice was now calm. Unlike some of her fellows, she had never hidden what she did from her daughter. "Are you okay?"

"Yes, fine. But I'm still in Tucson."

"Did you see my brothers?"

She glanced to Gabe and then to Clyne. "Yes." She gripped her neck with her opposite hand so hard that her back began to ache.

"I want to meet them!" Her daughter's voice filled with longing.

"Maybe soon."

And maybe forever. Cassidy's heart ached low down and deep, reminding her of a pain she had not felt since she'd discovered her husband had been killed in action.

She needed to get them out of Arizona. If only that would work. But she knew that moving wouldn't protect Amanda from one particular threat. The ICWA, Indian Child Welfare Act. Sovereign rights. Tribal rights.

"Are you listening to me?" asked Amanda.

"What was that, pumpkin?"

"I asked if you will be back in time for Saturday's game?"

She glanced to Clyne, the newest of the tribal council and enemy number one in her book. Oh, if she could just find something to bury them but all she'd come up with was something ancient on the third brother, Clay. She stiffened. A brow arched as she looked at Clyne, who narrowed his eyes at her.

"I'll try, pumpkin."

"Oh, Mom!"

From the phone, Cassidy heard the sound of a scoreboard buzzer.

"I've got to go."

Cassidy pictured her in her red-and-white basketball uniform, her dark hair pulled back in a ponytail, her lips tinted pink from the colored lip gloss her daughter had begun wearing.

It was her last year of elementary school. Her last year of eligibility in the youth basketball league. Next year Cassidy would have a teenager on her hands. She hoped.

"I love you," said Cassidy.

"You, too." The line went dead.

She held the phone to her chest for just a moment, eyes closed against the darkness that crept into her heart. What would she do if they took her daughter away?

"Was that her?"

The gruff male voice brought her about and she faced Clyne, who had snuck up on her without a sound.

Cassidy straightened for a fight with Clyne—her daughter's eldest brother and the first name on the complaint petitioning to have her daughter's closed adoption opened and overturned. She knew he'd win. He knew it, too. She saw not an ounce of pity for her in those deep brown eyes. Just the alert stare of a confident man facing a foe.

His face was all angles where her daughter's was all soft curves and the promise of the woman she would soon become.

An Apache woman. Not if she could help it. Amanda would be whatever she wanted and not be limited to one place and one clannish tribe who clung to that mountain as if it were more than just another outcropping of stone. Cold as his heart, she suspected. What did he know about Amanda, anyway? Nothing. According to his records he'd been deployed with the US Marines when his sister had been born and hadn't been discharged until after the accident that took his mother.

"Was that who?" she asked. But she knew. Still she made him say it.

"Jovanna?" he said, breathing the word, just a whisper.

Her skin prickled at the hushed intimate tone.

"Her name is Amanda Gail Walker."

"Amanda?" Clyne spat the word as he threw up his hands. "I've never met an Apache woman named Amanda."

"And you won't meet this one if I have any say in it."

"We are her family," said Clyne. "Her *real* family."

"Hey, I'm just as real as the family that didn't even know she was alive for twelve years."

"Nine," he corrected. Nine years on July 4 since his mother had died in that auto accident.

"If it were up to you all, she would have been raised in a series of group homes in South Dakota."

"You are not a mother. You're a field agent."

"And?"

"You have no husband, no other children."

"What's your point?"

"You are alone raising my sister and you have a very dangerous job. You were shot today! You could get killed at any moment. A good mother doesn't put her child at that kind of risk."

"It's an important job."

"So is motherhood," said Clyne. "So is teaching her who she is, who her people are, where she comes from. She belongs where her tribe has lived for centuries. You move her around like she's a canary."

"You finished? Because it isn't up to you. It's up to the judge. Until then I do my job and you keep away from *my* daughter."

"Walker!" She turned to see her boss closing in. "Outside. Now."

She followed him out into the hallway.

"What was that?" asked Tully.

"Custody battle," she said.

"I know all about that. What I'm asking about is why are you fighting with a tribal councilman?"

"Perhaps I'm not the right one for this assignment," she said, hating herself for saying it. She'd never turned down an assignment before.

"I agree. But I need an agent up there on Black Mountain. One who is not Apache and Chief Cosen just gave me an in. So you're it.

Find out what's going on up there. You got it? We've got permission for two agents on that rez. That's never happened before. So shut your mouth and do your job."

"Yes, sir." Cassidy had a thought. "Do you think the Cosens might be involved with the distribution ring?"

"How do I know? That's for you to find out."

Cassidy's mood brightened.

If she were up there, in his home, in his community, perhaps she could find some chink in the Cosen armor, something to make them unfit to raise a twelve-year-old child.

But if that were so, then why in the wide world would Chief Gabe Cosen allow her up in his territory?

She had a terrible thought. What if the Cosen brothers wanted her up there, away from the protection of other agents, so that something bad could happen to her? That would remove her from the equation when it came to the custody of her daughter.

Cassidy drew in a breath and faced her boss. It was a gamble. But it was the only way she could see to keep Amanda without putting her daughter in the position to choose.

A twelve-year-old should not have to choose between her mother and her brothers. It wasn't fair to ask a child to make such a choice. But Amanda would have to, if it came down to that.

Cassidy squared her shoulders as if she were still at attention in lineup. Then she met the analytical gaze of Donald Tully.

"If I do this, will you put in that recommendation for my transfer to DC?" she asked.

Tully's mouth went tight, but the glimmer in his eyes showed he knew she had won. "You know we do some good work here, too."

"Answer the question."

"Yes, damn it. I will."

"All right. I'll do it."

HIS BROTHER ANSWERED on the first ring.

"I got her!" he said, his voice full of jubilation.

"You sure?" asked his brother, Johnny.

"Gray Volvo station wagon, right?"

"That's what I said."

Johnny had tailed her the day she'd shown up in court to testify on a big case. She'd lost the tail easily but now they knew the make and model of her personal vehicle.

"She heading to the hospital?" Johnny asked.

"Don't know," he said.

"Damned, I hit her dead center. Should have knocked her down, at least. Then I would have had another shot," said Johnny.

"We need to get that tungsten ammo."

"We don't. Common caliber will get the job done."

"If it's a head shot."

"It was a head shot," said Johnny. "She moved. Jumped on him."

"What about a bigger caliber or a hollow point?"

"We buy that and we might as well wave a red flag in front of the Feds' eyes. No reason to buy that ammo but one."

"No guts, no glory," he said, using Johnny's favorite expression.

"Hey, I'm all about hitting the target. Just don't want a spot next to Brett's."

"What do you mean?"

"In the cemetery, stupid," said Johnny.

"Right," he said. Johnny was always the smart one. "She's heading for the interstate."

"Heading home, maybe. That'd be a break. Get her address if you can," said Johnny.

"Sure. Sure."

"Hey, kid? Finding her car? Ya done good."

He basked in the praise. Truth was, he didn't mind a cell next to Johnny's. Just so long as he took care of business first.

Chapter Four

Seemed you only needed to get shot to get the rest of the day off. Cassidy's boss sent her to the hospital. But she didn't go. Instead, she went home to her daughter. The drive from Tucson to Phoenix took three hours, but it didn't matter. She made it in time for supper.

She arrived with pizza and found Diane waiting with the table set. Amanda bounded off the couch and accepted a kiss and then the boxes, which she carried to the kitchen dinette.

Gerard's mother retrieved the milk from the refrigerator for Amanda and then took her seat. Diane had many good qualities. Cooking was not one of them. But she was the only other family Amanda had. Cassidy gritted her teeth at the lie. The only family that Cassidy wanted her to have. Was that selfish?

"Finally," said Diane. "I'm starving."

Diane was sixty-three, black and didn't look a day over fifty. She had taken an early retirement from UPS five years ago when her only son had been killed in action. Her skin was a lighter brown than her son's had been and she chose to straighten her hair, instead of leaving it natural, as Gerard had.

When Cassidy had transferred from California to Arizona, Diane had joined them. Her decision to help raise Amanda had allowed Cassidy to take Amanda out of the school keeper's programs and allowed Cassidy to move into fieldwork, which she truly loved.

Cassidy excused herself to change. Using a mirror, she checked the sight of the impact and noted the purplish bruise that spread across her back. She took four ibuprofens and slipped into a button-up blouse because it hurt too much to lift her arms over her head. Then she rejoined her mother-in-law and daughter.

After dinner it was past nine on a school night. Amanda headed off to bed. Cassidy joined her, sitting on the foot of the twin bed, trying not to look at the photo of her husband on his second deployment that rested on Amanda's nightstand.

"You're leaving again, aren't you?" said Amanda.

Cassidy stroked her daughter's glossy black

hair away from her face. Clyne's hair had been just this color. Gabe and Kino kept their hair so short it was hard to compare and she had yet to meet Clay, the middle brother.

"Yes, doodlebug. I have to pack tonight. I'll be gone before you get up."

"We have another game on Wednesday."

"I'm sorry."

"Where?" Her daughter knew that her mother couldn't say much about her assignments. But this time, somehow, it seemed important that she know.

"Black Mountain."

"On the reservation?" Her daughter's voice now rose with excitement. "Oh, Mom. Why didn't you tell me?"

Because she tried to keep her daughter away from the people who were attempting to take Amanda away from her.

"Can I come?"

"Of course you can't come."

Her daughter continued on and Cassidy wished she had not mentioned the location of her assignment.

"Are you going to Pinyon Fort? Will you see the museum? There are two hotels on Black Mountain, the ski resort and the casino. Where will you stay?"

It was like watching a train pick up speed and having no way to slow it down.

Ever since Cassidy had told her daughter that she was not really Sioux, as they had been told, but Apache, Amanda had been Googling the Black Mountain tribe's website and studying Apache history.

"I'm not sure yet." Cassidy pressed a hand to her forehead.

"You have to tell me everything, what it's like. They had snow there today. I checked. I haven't seen snow since we left South Dakota. I wish I could come, too."

Cassidy stroked her daughter's head and forced a smile.

"Maybe next time."

"Will you see them?"

"Yes."

Amanda's eyes widened. "Oh, I want to go!"

"I know."

"What if the judge says I have to go with them? Wouldn't it be better if I had at least met them?"

Cassidy's heart ached at the possibility of losing her daughter.

"They can't take you for long. Even if the judge overturns my custody, you remember what I told you?"

"I'm twelve."

Cassidy nodded.

Amanda recited by memory. "Twelve-year-olds can request to be adopted away from their tribe."

"That's right."

Amanda frowned. Ever since they'd discovered who she really was and that she had another family out there, Amanda had been increasingly unhappy. Of course the opening of her adoption and the challenge for custody upset her. Why wouldn't it?

"They can't win," said Cassidy. "Because you are old enough to choose."

Amanda moved her legs restlessly under the covers and seemed to want to say something.

Cassidy waited.

"Can you at least take a picture of them?"

"What? Why?"

"So I can see if they look like me?"

How she wished she could go back to the time when they both thought she had no one but her mom and dad and Grandma Diane. When there was no one else.

"I don't think that's a good idea," said Cassidy.

"Please?" asked Amanda.

Cassidy tucked the covers back in place. "I have to go pack and you have to go to sleep. Good night, sweetheart."

Amanda kissed her mother and then flopped to her side. She said nothing more as Cassidy walked to the bedroom door and waited.

She was about to give up when Amanda flopped back to face her.

"Be careful up there, Mom."

"I will. I love you."

"You, too."

Cassidy closed the door and headed to her bedroom to pack. She was good at packing. A tour of duty with the US Army had taught her that. And also how to fly helicopters. She'd put in for a transfer from her first assignment with the FBI after Gerard died because she couldn't stand to live in the home they had chosen together. They'd ended up in Southern California.

After she had finished in her room, she carried her suitcase, briefcase and duffel down to the hallway. She told Diane all she could about where she was going. But she didn't tell her that after this assignment she would finally get her transfer. Would Diane come with them or would it be just the two of them again?

She didn't know. What she did know was she needed the custody decision so that Amanda could tell the judge she wanted to be adopted again by her mother. Then she needed to get away from this part of the country. As far as possible from the Apache tribe. Until then, she was keeping her daughter away from the Cosen brothers.

"So you won't change your mind?" Clyne asked Gabe.

"Do you know how many officers I have?"

Clyne did, of course. Twelve officers for twenty-six hundred square miles. Only it was eleven since he'd lost a man in January.

"I need help, Clyne. Not just on processing evidence in the Arizona crime labs. I need investigators. Because if you think this is over with you are mistaken. All we did was slow them down. They'll be back and I don't want my guys killed in gun battles with Mexican cartel killers."

Clyne did not want that, either.

"But why her?" He meant Agent Walker.

"Do you know anything about her?"

"All I need to know."

"That's bull. She's highly qualified and she knows what she is doing. She knows all the players. You have to trust me on this."

Clyne tried for humor. "She's a real company man, huh? She probably wears that FBI T-shirt to bed."

That gave him a strong image of pale legs peeking out from beneath a navy blue T-shirt that ended right below her slender hips.

Clyne growled. He stood with his four brothers, all now wrapped in blankets and perched as close to the fire as possible as their uncle Luke added the stones to the fire. The stones were among the Great Spirit's creations and so had a life force and power like all things in nature. Luke would be tending the fire and passing the hot stones into their wikiup for the ceremony of purification. Their uncle was the only one dressed appropriately for the chilly night air, warm enough to unzip his parka and remove his gloves.

"When will she be here?" he asked.

His uncle took that one. "Tomorrow morning. Late morning, I think. In time for the BIA presentation."

Their people had a love-hate relationship with the Bureau of Indian Affairs, who oversaw business on the reservation for the federal government. But the BIA had money Clyne needed for their water treatment facility so he would do his best to play nice.

Luke poked at the coals, judging the heat. "Almost ready."

Clyne began to shiver and Clay was now jumping up and down to keep warm.

Kino nudged between Clay and Gabe. He still had a white bandage on his throat. A visible reminder of how close they had been to losing him. Clyne remembered Gabe's words about not wanting to lose any more officers to this war with traffickers. He knew from Gabe that his men had been outgunned. The cartel killers had automatic weapons and the tribal police force was issued rifles, shotguns and sidearms. It was not a fair fight.

Clyne looked from Gabe to Kino. Would the FBI presence on the rez help keep them safe or put them at greater risk?

"Will she bring Jovanna?" asked Kino.

Gabe cast him an impatient look. "She doesn't want her to meet us."

"But the attorney says we'll win," said Kino. "Any day and we'll win."

"And she'll slap a petition to allow Jovanna to choose to be adopted," said Clay. "Our attorney said so."

"Nothing we can do about that," said Gabe.

They all looked to Clyne, as they had since he'd came home from the endless fighting in the Middle East to assume his place as head of this household.

"We have a petition, too. I spoke to our attorney yesterday."

Before he was almost killed. She wouldn't do something like that. Set him up, would she? Killing him wouldn't stop this. She must know that.

"Our sister can't make a fair choice unless she has had an opportunity to meet us," said Clyne.

Clay grinned. "Think that will work?"

"I do. It's logical. It's appropriate."

"How long will we have her?" asked Kino.

A lifetime, Clyne hoped. His sister belonged here with them in the place of their ancestors.

"I've asked for a year," said Clyne.

Kino gave a whistle.

Luke poked at the stones. "You boys ready?"

They shucked off their blankets and ducked into the domed structure. All of the brothers had built this sweat lodge. The stone foundation lined the hollow they dug into the earth and the saplings arched beneath the bark-and-leather covering.

Clay and Kino moved to sit across the nest of fresh pinon pine and cedar branches. Clyne was glad the two had somehow managed to leave their pretty new wives for the evening to join their elder brothers in the sweat lodge.

Outside the entrance to the east, the sacred fire burned. Their uncle would stand watch, providing hot stones, protecting the ceremony.

Clyne sat in a breechclout made from white cotton. Both Gabe and Kino preferred loose gym shorts and Clay sat in his boxers, having forgotten his shorts. Luke passed in the first stone, using a forked cedar branch. Clyne moved it to the bed of sage, filling the lodge with the sweet scent. More stones followed as Clyne and his brothers began to sing. When the stones were all in place Luke dropped the flap to cover the entrance and the lodge went dark, black as a cave, the earth, a womb, the place where they had come from and would one day return. Here their voices joined as they sang their prayer.

Gabe used a horn cup to pour the water of life over the stone people, the ones who came before Changing Woman made the Apache from her skin.

Steam rose all about them and their voices blended as sweat ran from their bodies with the impurities. Clyne breathed in the scent of sweet pine and cedar and prayed for the return of their sister.

Chapter Five

Cassidy Walker called ahead so the tribal police wouldn't pull her over like they did the last time. She made it to Black Mountain but did not have time to make it to her room at the Black Mountain Casino. This was one of two hotels on the property. The other was clear up in Wind River where the tribe had a ski resort, but that was too far from Clyne's home.

From her former partner, she knew the Cosens all lived near the main town. Clyne and Gabe lived with their mother Tessa's mother, Glendora Clawson. Both the younger brothers were newlyweds and had their own homes. Kino was expecting his first child.

Amanda is about to become an aunt.

The realization came like a kick to her gut.

It didn't matter, she told herself. That petition would hit the minute the judge ruled. A week or two up here in the hinterland and she'd have her promotion. The judge would rule against her but the petition would reverse Amanda's placement. In six months she and her daughter would be living in DC or lower Manhattan. One thing was certain, Amanda would have an education and opportunities she would not likely receive on the reservation. Amanda would have the chance to become whatever she wished.

The ringing phone made her jump clear out of her seat. The ID said it was Tully. She hit the speak button on her phone.

"Good morning, sir."

"You there yet?"

"Nearly." She had decided to catch a few hours' sleep at home and leave at five in the morning, rather than drive up last night as Tully had suggested. "Anything on the shooting?"

She couldn't help stretching and then winced. Sitting made her ribs hurt. Breathing made her ribs hurt. Talking made her ribs hurt. She glanced at the ibuprofen bottle and then the clock. One more hour before she could have another dose.

"Yes. One shooter, .30 caliber. Positioned on the Star of Tucson Hotel. We now have three cartridges. Forensics has everything we could pull from up there. Garbage mostly, we think. But maybe we'll get a hit."

"Let's hope," she said.

"Change of plans for today."

Cassidy tensed. She didn't like surprises and so tried to be ready for every eventuality. But she hadn't seen this assignment coming. That was certain.

"Gabe Cosen called. His brother has a ground-breaking on the rez today. He wants you and Forrest on hand in case there is trouble."

"I thought we were up here to pursue leads to apprehend Ronald Hare and investigate the—"

Her boss cut in. "Yeah. Yeah. But today try to be sure Cosen doesn't get shot." He provided her with the coordinates given to him by Police Chief Cosen. "Clyne Cosen has another rally off-reservation in Phoenix on Wednesday. Damned victory tour. You and Forrest are accompanying him from Black Mountain to the rally."

"Does he know this?"

"Not yet."

Cassidy grimaced. This wasn't going to be good. She knew Clyne Cosen well enough to know that. But she also didn't like the bait and switch. She was here to investigate the ongoing drug activity here. Not play nursemaid to a bristly Apache who didn't want her within a mile of him.

"We'll be on-site for the next rally. This one

is indoors, so no BS. Love to find the shooter before then."

"You and me both." She couldn't help but twist to check the sore muscles and ribs. Yup. They still hurt. "I'm here. Gotta go."

"Check in after the event."

"Yes, sir." She disconnected and said, "And keep that transfer request front and center."

Cassidy pulled into the barren patch of ground her GPS had brought her to. She would have been certain she was off course but there was a series of fluttering triangular flags flapping briskly in the March breeze. She dragged her winter coat from the rear seat. Down in Phoenix it was sixty degrees. But up here fourteen thousand feet above sea level there was ice on the ground.

"That's why they call themselves Mountain Apache," she muttered.

A leaning white sign advertised the future site of the Black Mountain water treatment facility. *Whoo-hoo*, she thought and climbed from the vehicle. The wind tore a strand of hair from her ponytail and no amount of recovery could make it stay in place. Her chin-length hair was just too short for a pony and she'd be damned if she'd be seen outside the house in either pigtails or a headband.

She glanced at her watch and saw she'd arrived forty-five minutes early. That gave her time to check the perimeter and to wish she had worn thicker socks. The open field left few places to hide and the lack of any obvious vehicle was encouraging. But with a scope, a shooter could easily be in range. Clyne had agreed to wear body armor for this event. Cassidy adjusted hers, her backup. The one without the distortion over her heart.

Back at her sedan, Cassidy was just lifting her phone to call Luke when a line of vehicles, mostly pickups, arrived in a long train of bright color. The wind pushed her forward and she had to widen her stance to keep from losing her footing. The sudden movement made her ribs ache.

She watched the men and women emerge from their vehicles. Clyne was easy to spot. She didn't know exactly why. Perhaps his height or the crisp way he walked. He joined some men dressed in trenches, walking with them along the flapping flags.

Luke walked slightly behind them. She knew the instant Clyne spotted her because his ready smile dipped with his brow. Then he turned his attention back to his conversation with his guests.

She heard him say, "Self-sustaining and by

using local labor we expect to come in below the estimate."

She fell into stride behind him, ignoring the heady scent of pine that reached her as Clyne passed. He'd smelled like that yesterday, she recalled, when he had carried her into the hotel. Cassidy inhaled deeply, enjoying the appealing fragrance.

"Hey," said Luke.

"How was last night?" she asked.

"Quiet. You?"

"Good."

"What did they say at the hospital?"

She didn't answer.

"Cassidy?"

She fessed up. "I went home."

Luke's smile seemed sad. He had met Amanda more than once in the times before she knew he was her uncle. Amanda's father's half brother. If it were only him, she wouldn't mind Amanda getting to know him better. Luke, she knew and trusted.

"I got Gabe to put someone on Manny Escalanti. Told him our office would pick up the overtime."

Manny Escalanti was the new head of the Wolf Posse, the Apache gang operating on the rez. It had been this gang that had held the chemicals for production and moved the mobile meth labs to keep them ahead of tribal police.

"We need ears on him, too. Do we know if the Mexican cartels are still working with them?"

"DOJ says that they are working with both the Salt River gang and the Wolf Posse."

In January, the cartel had decided to move operations to Salt River but failed to capture the chemicals needed because Gabe and his very connected fiancée, Selena Dosela, had succeeded in stopping them. Selena was also Black Mountain Apache and her father, Frasco, had ties to the Wolf Posse and American distributor, Cesaro Raggar. Good thing Dosela was working with them now.

"What do you think of Selena?" she asked.

"I think she's very brave and very lucky."

"I mean, do you think she is working with the cartels?"

"No. Not at all."

His answer was a little too quick as if that was what he hoped to be true, rather than what was true.

"Her father was recruited by Raggar."

Raggar was the head of the American distribution operation running the business from federal prison.

"And Frasco went to DOJ and made a deal."

"To save his hide," said Cassidy.

"It's a valid reason to come to us. Kept his family safe and got them out of the operation."

"Unless Raggar retaliates."

"Gabe is very worried about that. Even asked me about witness protection for Selena's entire family."

That was new information.

"But her father won't leave the rez."

The sentiment seemed endemic up here, she thought.

The group formed a rough circle around nothing she could see other than that this was the place that their tribal councilman had chosen to stop moving forward into the barren field.

She and Forrest stepped back, just outside the circle, scanning the audience and the surrounding area.

"Too far from cover," she said to Forrest.

"Too cold, as well. We won't be out long."

But it didn't take long for a bullet to travel through a person's flesh and bone.

Cassidy scanned the faces, checked the hands and listened to Clyne lift his voice to describe the fantastical water treatment plant as if it were some shining tower sitting on a hill instead of a pit that strained excrement.

Cassidy scanned the faces and realized that she and the two representatives from the BIA,

Bureau of Indian Affairs, were the only white people in the gathering.

Clyne spoke loud enough for the gathering to hear and she had to admit his argument for the funding was eloquent, thoughtful and timely, but perhaps wasted on the men who were wearing the equivalent of raincoats in the unceasing wind. They stomped their feet restlessly as she swept the crowd, impressed with the practical clothing of the rest of the gathering.

Clyne finished and the men all shook hands. Photos were taken for the Black Mountain webpage and Cassidy made sure she was not in any of them. The procession retreated to the string of vehicles that reminded her of a wagon train for some reason. She shadowed Clyne to his vehicle where he stopped to glare at her.

"Would you like me to follow you or accompany you?"

"Neither," said Clyne.

"Then I'll follow." She stepped away so he could open his door. "Shouldn't Gabe be here, too?"

He smirked at her and just that simple upturning of his mouth made her insides twitch in a most unwelcome physical reaction to a man in whom she refused to have any interest.

"He is here. He told me to tell you that you did a pretty good job of scouting the perimeter.

Though not too good, obviously." With that he climbed in the navy blue pickup and swung the door closed.

The truck rode high, leaving her at shoulder level with the decal of the great seal of the Black Mountain tribe that was affixed to the door panel and showed a chunk missing at the top right. The seal included Black Mountain in the background with a pine tree, eagle feather and something that looked like a brown toadstool in the foreground.

"Try and keep up," he said and led the procession back toward town, leaving her to scurry along the icy shoulder to reach her vehicle. Her time in South Dakota had taught her about driving in snow, but she still skidded on the icy patch as she pulled into place. Clearly Clyne was as thrilled at her current assignment as she was. Somehow she didn't think that commonality would bring them any closer together. If she could just find something that would connect the Cosens to the mobile meth ring or something that made their home unfit, she could challenge custody, collect her transfer and be on her way.

She made the drive at the end of the snake of cars, parked in the lot beside tribal headquarters and followed the remains of the procession inside, where she was asked to present her credentials, sign in and wear a paper name badge.

Hi, My Name Is... Pissed Off, she thought.

Gabe Cosen appeared through the doors and paused only to speak to the receptionist in Apache before coming to meet her.

"Agent Walker. Nice to see you again."

She accepted his offered hand. The handshake was firm and brief. Chief Cosen stepped back from her. Gabe had none of his brother's swagger. He had bedroom eyes that made Cassidy uneasy and the same full mouth as Clyne. But his gaze was completely different. She saw no hint of distain or banked resentment.

"Chief Cosen. I understand this isn't the first time you have seen me today."

"That's true." Chief Cosen grinned and she felt nothing. Why did Clyne's attention stir her up like ice in a blender?

Chief Cosen removed his gray Stetson and gave it a spin on one hand. His hair was cut very short, which was so different from the long, managed braids of his older brother.

"Police headquarters is right across the street. I'm going to get you and Luke set up right after lunch. Say one o'clock?"

"That's fine."

"I've got to speak to Clyne. Would you mind?" He motioned for her to accompany him.

She forced a smile. Why had she been hoping she would not have to see Clyne again today?

Cassidy kept pace with Gabe as they walked down the hall and through the outer offices of the tribal council. She resisted the urge to look at Clyne through the bank of glass that skirted the door to his office.

Gabe paused before the assistant's desk. The Apache woman sat with her legs slightly splayed to accommodate her swollen belly. Cassidy thought she looked ready to deliver at any moment. The woman held the phone wedged between her ear and shoulder as she wrote something on a memo pad. She still had time to lift a finger to Gabe in a silent request that he wait.

Gabe stepped back and faced Cassidy.

"You settling in?" asked Gabe.

"I haven't been to the casino hotel yet."

"Oh, it was my understanding that you would arrive last night."

"Personal business. Delayed."

His smile faded. "Of course. How are you feeling?"

She shifted testing her ribs and felt the sting of healing muscle. "Fine."

He peered at her from under his brow and she felt he did not quite believe her.

"Well. On behalf of myself and my family, I

want to thank you personally for protecting our older brother yesterday."

The display of manners, so divergent from those of his older brother, shocked her into speechlessness.

"Ah," she struggled. "You're welcome."

"Strange, don't you think, that you would be the one responsible for his protection?"

Was there an accusation there or a hint of suspicion?

"It was a rotation."

"Yes. So I understand." Gabe didn't try to hold on to his smile.

"I thought you'd be more present today," she said.

"Clyne didn't want the BIA feeling unsafe."

Had she and Luke been too obvious? She didn't think the BIA officials even noticed her.

"He's been courting them for months and was afraid my force would raise questions about security. He has another rally tomorrow. Phoenix this time. Then Friday, some folks from a home-building charity visiting. Another outdoor gathering, touring the proposed building site here on Black Mountain."

"So you don't want help with the investigation. You asked for us to protect your brother?"

"No. I need investigators. But someone just

tried to kill Clyne yesterday. I could use the help keeping him safe."

"But why me, specifically?"

He watched her for a moment that stretched on to eternity.

"Can't you guess?"

"I don't like guessing games, Chief Cosen. Any games, really."

"Miss Walker, you have been a mother to my sister for most of her life. Perhaps the only mother she remembers. It seemed to me that we should know something about you and that you might want to know something about us."

She knew all she needed to know about them, or wanted to. "This has nothing to do with the investigation."

"It does. But two birds, so to speak."

"Do your brothers feel the same?"

Gabe rubbed the back of his neck and she had her answer.

"Gabe!" Clyne's voice was much louder than it needed to be when he called from the open door.

"Excuse me." Gabe stepped into his brother's office and shut the door.

She could hear their words but did not understand Apache. The angry voices and the flailing arm gestures were clear enough as both men engaged in an epic battle of wills.

Gabe eventually reached for the knob. Clyne stood with both fists planted on the surface of his desk. Gabe cleared the threshold and planted his hat on his head. His breathing was fast and his nostrils flared as he turned his attention to her.

"My brother would like to take you to lunch," he said.

The office assistant lifted her brows at this announcement and glanced from Gabe to Cassidy still waiting.

"I was meeting Luke for lunch."

"He told me that he will see you after lunch," said Gabe.

Cassidy reached for her phone and sent Luke a text. The reply was immediate.

C U after lunch.

Cassidy squared her shoulders and marched into the lion's den.

Chapter Six

Clyne looked back to Field Agent Walker, who glared at him from the outer office, her eyes now glinting like sunlight on a blue gemstone. She held her navy parka in her lap, because he had not offered to hang it and wore a blazer, presumably a different one. One without a bullet hole in the back. Her drab gray button-up shirt did not quite hide the flak jacket beneath, and her practical lace-up nylon boots showed salt stains on the toes. Fully erect, she didn't even reach Clyne's chin. Her blond hair had again been yanked back into a severe ponytail but the March wind had tugged the side strands away and they now floated down about her pink face. If she were Swedish, he did not think her skin could be any paler. Outwardly, they were completely different, but they had one thing in common. They were both fighters. So why did his chest ache every time he forced himself to look at her?

She seemed ready to spit nails. He lifted one of the fists he had been braced upon from his desk and motioned her forward as a Tai Chi master summoned his next challenger.

Walker's fine golden brow arched and her pointed chin dipped. He lowered his chin as well, as one ram does when preparing to butt heads with another. He thought he welcomed the fight, but her proximity raised a completely different kind of anticipation. He identified the curling tension of sexual desire and nearly groaned out loud. Not for this woman. No. Absolutely not.

Her stride was staccato and devoid of any female wiles. So why was he breathing so fast?

Now he noticed how her eyes seemed not quite sapphire, but more ocean blue and flashing like a thunderstorm.

She marched into his office with her coat clutched at her left hip, leaving her gun hand free.

"Just so we are clear," said Clyne, "I haven't changed my mind."

"Good afternoon to you, too, Councilman."

He ground his teeth. Something about her made him forget his manners. He had a reputation for charm but this woman stripped away that veneer like paint thinner on varnish. He felt about as enchanting as a prickly cactus. He glared at her, deciding if he should retreat, advance or return her greeting.

"I don't need protection," he said.

"I have a slug in my body armor that says otherwise."

"That was down there in your world."

She lifted a brow. "Well, I really don't own the whole thing. I'm just a renter."

He scowled because if he didn't he feared he might laugh.

"So do you want to tell me if your problem is with my world, the FBI or just me?"

"You don't have that kind of time."

"Try me." She folded her arms and braced against the door frame.

"Well, let's start with single white women adopting poor little Indian children."

She sucked in a breath as his first blow struck home. "I was married when we adopted our daughter."

That announcement set him back and he didn't think he hid the surprise. Clyne quickly reevaluated. He'd assumed she was one of those career women who wanted it all and had decided that if she didn't want the physical inconvenience of being pregnant, she could just buy a baby.

"Was?" he said.

FBI personal records were sealed. Even Gabe, the tribal police chief, could find very little information about her. That put him at a disadvantage here because she likely knew a great deal about him. Perhaps his brother was right. They should know what kind of a woman had raised their sister.

Was she one of those modern women who thought life came as an all-you-could-eat buffet? Clyne knew better. Life was all about difficult choices.

Should he press or drop it? He studied her body language, arms folded, legs crossed at the ankle as she braced against the solid wooden frame. She was in full-out protective mode. But he was off balance now, fighting with a hand tied behind his back.

"Yes, was," she said.

"So you are now unmarried?"

She inclined her head like a queen consenting to give a response.

"But you have sole custody. Jovanna's only guardian?" asked Clyne, refusing to use the word *parent* as he considered the possibility of having to go through another custody battle with her husband.

"Guardian? I'm her mother. And yes, I am her sole guardian."

"Then you should take a desk job," he said. Her flashing eyes made it clear what she thought of his suggestion.

"Risk comes with living. Your mother's death should have taught you that. And this reservation doesn't have magic properties. You're not safe hiding up here on this mountain, either."

"We aren't hiding. We're living and we choose to be separate. To preserve our culture and teach our children where they come from and who they are." Even to his own ears his words sounded like a speech given from rote.

She had uncrossed her arms and now tilted her head. Her hair shone yellow as corn silk. He saw something in her eyes.

"Doing fabulously well by all accounts. What's the teen pregnancy rate now?"

"Irrelevant."

"Not if you have a teenage daughter it isn't. And where you come from is not as important as where you end up," she said. He'd heard the sentiment before, frequently from those who did not know where they came from or needed to forget. Which was she? A terrible childhood or one without roots?

"Does she even know about us?" he asked.

Her eyes narrowed and that cool demeanor slipped. "She does."

"And about the challenge?"

"Yes, again."

What did Jovanna think about that, to learn she was not an orphan but had an entire family waiting for her? Did she feel betrayed that they had not come for her sooner?

They had gotten little information from their attorney about their sister's life. Mainly facts. Nothing that would tell him how she felt or if she had been happy.

Jovanna had been removed from the vehicle after their mother's death by a state trooper, who had turned her over to child welfare, who had seen her in her dance competition dress and turned her over to BIA. The trooper's writing, "One survivor," had been transposed to read "No survivors" and they had learned, incorrectly, that they had lost both their mother and sister to a drunk driver.

Jovanna had disappeared into the system. Only after their grandmother had insisted they place a stone lamb on Jovanna's grave to mark her tenth birthday, had they learned that only their mother was buried in that grave. The search had begun. He had flown to South Dakota and hired an investigator. Gabe had used his badge to get more information. Kino had followed the procedures to open the adoption and Clay now waited for a ruling from the judge on their motion.

But during those nine years, Jovanna had been listed as a member of the Sweetgrass tribe of Sioux Indians. No kin had come forward, so she was placed in an orphanage at age two and then in a foster home with a Sioux family at age three. Then Jovanna had been adopted just after she turned four.

"We want to meet her," said Clyne.

Her hand settled on the grip of her pistol and her eyes met his. "No."

"Why not?"

"Because it will only make it harder when we leave."

Leave? Where was she going? And then he remembered what his uncle had said about his new partner. A hotshot. A firecracker. Destined to be promoted and transferred to a major field office. And if that happened, they might lose Jovanna again.

"You're leaving?" he asked.

She nodded. "Just as soon and as far from here as possible."

He took a step in her direction, leaving the authority of his desk. She sidestepped until she was beyond his grasp. He lifted his top from the coat rack, his attention still on her. She rolled those crystal-blue eyes at him and exhaled.

"My brother says I am to take you to lunch."

Cassidy did not like the twinkle in his eyes

one little bit. But she was a guest here and if Chief Cosen wanted her to dine with his brother, she could do that. She wondered if anyone else found that funny.

"You ready?" he asked.

She lifted her arms, still bundled in her jacket. "Seems so."

He motioned to the door but she waited. "After you, Councilman."

Clyne turned to his assistant. "I'll be at Catalina's," he said and headed out the door, leaving Cassidy no choice but to follow.

In the large foyer before the great seal she paused to zip her coat, realized she would not be able to reach her weapon and left it unfastened.

"Who is Catalina?" she asked.

"Not who. What," he answered.

"I'll drive," she said.

"Why?"

"Everyone knows your SUV."

He made a sound that could have been a laugh. "They all know your dark federal-issue sedan, too, Agent Walker. Besides, it's only across the street."

"Walking out in the open. Bad idea," she said.

"You want to drive? Go ahead."

"I want you inside a vehicle and eating in a securable location. I don't know this place and we have no protection there."

"Oh, but I have you, Agent Walker," he said.

"You can call me Cassidy."

He shot her that wary look again.

"If you want."

Clyne looked like he didn't want to call her by her first name. But he nodded and then set out the door.

She followed his directions to Catalina's, which turned out to be a little diner tucked across the street and behind the main road so as to be invisible to outsiders. The exterior was humble enough, with peeling paint and large tinted windows. Cassidy knew that she would have been apt to avoid entering had Clyne not marched up the stairs, leaving her to follow.

The first thing that hit her was the aroma of frying bacon, onions and coffee, all mingled in an enticing mix that made her stomach rumble. She paused on the welcome mat to scan the room for potential threats. The place was alive with working men, seated at the counter, in booths. Men and women ate breakfast and lunch at the center circular tables. The interior was bright, large and had a central wood-burning stove that warmed the room and filled the air with the inviting scent of wood smoke.

The waitress called a greeting that she could not understand and Clyne responded in kind. He paused to speak to most of the men at the counter, patting some on the back and joking with others. But he spoke in Apache, leaving her unable to follow what was said. Each man turned to glance at her, stone-faced, eyebrows lifted. In all her travels, she had never felt so aware of her white skin, pale hair and European lineage. Clyne worked the room, settling at last in a central table by the woodstove.

The waitress arrived with a smile for Clyne and a scowl for Cassidy. She thought it was Clyne's intention to unsettle her, so she scanned the room once more and then studied the menu. It was in Apache. She blew away her frustration and set it back behind the salt and pepper shakers.

"That's what it feels like for us out there," he said. "Being a cultural outsider, feeling apart."

"But you choose to live apart."

His smile was cold, so why did it warm her insides?

"Well, don't take it personally."

She couldn't hold his gaze. It was too intense and made her all jittery inside. This was just terrible. In all her years she'd never had a crush on her assignment. But Clyne was different from anyone she'd ever met. Seemingly charming, but beneath that *protective* exterior, she sensed danger and inner strength. A heady combination, she admitted.

She lifted her gaze to catch him watching her in a way that made her insides tense.

"What would you like? I'll order for you."

She told him and he placed the order. The waitress, an older woman dressed in jeans and a T-shirt that depicted a string of armed Apache warriors and read Homeland Security, Fighting Terrorism Since 1492.

Their coffee arrived and Cassidy sipped the strong brew and sighed.

"You have me at a disadvantage, Cassidy," Clyne said. "You know a great deal about me. I know little about you."

"I thought you didn't want to know anything about me."

"I didn't. But Gabe is right. You have raised my sister."

"I'm not talking about Amanda."

"Fine. Your ex-husband, then."

He'd picked the topic that cut most deeply into her heart, but she'd be damned if she'd show him that.

"What about him?" She braced for the barrage.

"Why did you two decide to adopt?"

Personal business. But she answered. "We couldn't have children. We tried. Saw someone. But he couldn't…" She shrugged. Gerard was infertile. It had been hard to believe, so hard, when he was so virile and so… She flushed as she realized Clyne was watching her again.

"So you two decided to adopt an Indian child."

She met Clyne's gaze and held it as she delivered the next part of her answer. "We wanted a baby, like everyone else. Boy or girl, we didn't care."

"So why Jovanna? She wasn't a baby."

"They said she was between three and four."

Cassidy thought back, remembering the little girl she had been. She had looked at Gerard and then at Cassidy and made up her mind. How could they say no?

"She came up to us when we toured the facility. She was outgoing even then. And charming, like you."

His eyebrows lifted. She hadn't meant to say that.

Cassidy sipped the coffee and tried again. "She walked right up to Gerard and took his hand. She said…well, it doesn't matter. She picked us and stole our hearts all in the same instant."

Clyne cocked her head. "What did his family think about his adopting an Indian into his Anglo family?"

Now it was Cassidy's turn to scowl. She reached in her coat and withdrew her billfold.

She didn't carry a purse. Just did like her fellows. Wallet, cell phone, personal weapon, handcuffs and shield. What else did a girl need?

She drew out the photo she kept of Gerard's official portrait taken just before his second deployment. She liked this one because he'd managed to sneak a slight smile in past the army photographers. She also liked it because he was in his captain's uniform. Cassidy slipped it from the vinyl shield and passed it to Clyne.

"This is Gerard."

She watched as his eyes rounded and his gaze flicked to her and then back to the photo. "He's...an army captain."

She chuckled at how he'd avoided saying "black." Then she accepted the photo. It still hurt to look at Gerard's image, but the hurt was softer now, like a tug on her heart instead of a knife blade. She tucked away the photo.

"Captain and a tank commander. And to answer your question, Gerard's mother loved Amanda on sight. Diane moved out here to help me."

She had a grandmother, he realized. Two. His and Gerard's.

"When did you two break up?" asked Clyne.

She scowled, refusing to answer that one. He waited and then tried again.

"Why did you choose the name Amanda?"

Back on less rocky ground, Cassidy gave him a reply.

"She's called Amanda because that was what she called herself when she arrived into the care of the BIA."

"She never could say it right. Avana. That's what she called herself."

"Avana. Amanda," said Cassidy.

"What did she say to you that first meeting?"

She had said that she didn't want to speak of Amanda and here they were talking about her. She resisted but something in his gaze, something like pleading that he would never voice, made her relent.

"She hugged Gerard's leg and called him 'Daddy.' You should have seen him melt. Then she took his hand and my hand. I looked at Gerard and he nodded. We signed the papers that day."

"Just like that?"

"No. We also turned down the three-month-old we came to see. We didn't pick Amanda. She picked us."

He seemed about to say something when their meal arrived. Clyne handed back the photo.

The waitress set Clyne's food before him and slid hers over, letting Cassidy know that she was not happy to serve her.

She thanked the waitress, who said nothing to

her. Then Cassidy surveyed the offering. She'd stuck to the familiar, eggs, bacon, fried potatoes and white toast. She inhaled and glanced at Clyne's meal. Before him sat a large bowl of a rich aromatic stew and something that looked like the fried dough from the Italian festival she and Amanda once attended in San Diego.

"What's that?"

"Fry bread. Traditional Apache food. Try it."

"Is it sweet?" she asked, thinking of the powdered sugar that covered the Italian fried dough.

Clyne made a face. "No. Sometimes we put chili or other foods on top, like this beef stew. It's best hot." He motioned for her to take some.

She lifted her knife and fork preparing to cut away a bit as if it were an oversize pancake. He batted her hand away and took hold of the golden brown amorphous bread before tearing it into two pieces.

"Like this." He dipped it in his stew and took a bite. Then he dipped the smaller piece and offered it to her.

She took it and their hands brushed. Cassidy felt the tingle of awareness dart up her arm and right to her center. Her eyes widened and her gaze flashed to his to see his jaw had gone rock hard. His brow sank over his beautiful eyes and the tingling awareness squeezed her heart.

What the heck was this?

Clyne pulled away, leaving Cassidy holding the bread in the air as if it were a telegram portending bad news. She lifted the fry dough to her mouth and took a small bite. He watched her chew and swallow. The veins in his forehead appeared. Her mouth went dry.

"It's very good." Cassidy noticed the silence. She glanced about to see the room was also watching. Judging her?

Clyne turned his attention to his meal.

"I'm glad you enjoy it."

Cassidy focused on her meal as well, finishing in record time under the watchful stares of their audience.

The check arrived and she made a grab for it. Clyne was quicker and her hand landed on his. She drew back so fast her chair rocked. It didn't matter. The contact still made her insides twitch. This had happened once before, with Gerard, but it had developed slowly, over weeks. This was more visceral and much more immediate.

Cassidy stared at Clyne Cosen.

Oh, no. Please not this man.

Chapter Seven

Clyne left Cassidy at the tribal police offices across the street. For reasons he did not wish to examine, he walked her in to Gabe's office. He told himself it was only to prove that he had done as he promised, kept a civil tone and shared a meal with Agent Cassidy Walker. He didn't understand why Gabe thought this necessary. But it occurred to Clyne that instead of fighting Gabe on this, he should try to figure out what his brother, who had good reasons for his actions, was thinking.

Unfortunately his uncle and Gabe's second in command, Randall Juris, were both there. Detective Juris glanced at them through the glass windows that fronted his brother's office. Juris looked from Clyne to Cassidy and his brows lifted. Juris had once been a Hollywood stuntman and extra in various movies that needed Native American actors. His big barrel chest, dark skin and classic features made him the perfect foil to the Texas Rangers, settlers and scouts he had failed to best on camera. The truth was he could have bested any of them.

Cassidy paused outside the door to make use of the watercooler to assist in downing three brown tablets. She made a face and then shifted her shoulders. It was the first time that she'd given any indication that she'd taken a bullet yesterday. He knew how that felt, with and without a vest.

"Is that because of yesterday?" asked Clyne.

Cassidy shrugged and winced. "Just sore."

"Well, here she is!" The female voice came from behind them.

Clyne recognized the familiar new arrival and groaned. His grandmother was bustling across the room toward his open door. Cassidy turned toward this smiling stranger, noted she was the target of his grandmother's advance and wisely retreated two steps. She had time to crush the paper cup in her hand and drop it into the basket on the floor before his grandmother reached them.

Glendora Clawson was sixty-nine but looked somewhere in her fifties. Her hair, which was mostly black, brushed her shoulders and she had a wide grin on her broad face. Her pink snow coat was open, revealing a plump body dressed in black slacks and a cardigan sweater with a silver dragonfly pin affixed to her powder-pink blouse.

Cassidy backed into the wall of windows in her attempt to avoid his grandmother's arms now wrapping her up like a mama bear. Clyne smiled in amusement as Cassidy Walker stiffened. Behind her the audience of Forrest, Juris and his brother watched the unfolding drama like fans in a skybox.

Clyne met Gabe's eye and thought his brother was smiling. Clyne had a sneaking suspicion that this was also his brother's fault.

Glendora stepped back, her dark brows lifted high on her forehead. Then she turned her attention to Clyne.

"Why didn't you call me? I had to hear from Gabe that Cassidy was here." She said the name so casually as if she had the right to call Agent Walker by her first name, as if they were old acquaintances.

"She is here on business," said Clyne. None of them had told their grandmother that someone had shot at him yesterday. The woman had lost her husband and her only daughter. That seemed enough pain to them all.

"Nonsense. You are both coming for supper tonight. I'm making a roast."

"We can't," said Clyne, but the sinking feeling already gripped him. He'd rather face a nest of rattlers than have this woman seated at his family table.

"You will," said Glendora, lifting a brow in his direction.

Cassidy looked from one to the other. Cassidy shrugged and he nodded. Her face went grim for a moment but then she forced a smile and turned to his grandmother.

"I'd be honored," she said.

It was exactly what she should have said in this situation and Clyne knew it could not have been easy for her. His interest increased as he watched her with his grandmother.

"Gabe and Selena will be there. Lea and Kino. Clay and Izzie."

And he and the FBI agent that wanted sole custody of his sister. Seemed like a date from hell to him. His only consolation was that it would be worse on Cassidy.

He had to give Agent Walker some credit. She was cordial and warm to his grandmother. Her smile changed her entire demeanor and had him scowling. It was just not possible for him to find this fierce little warrior woman attractive. But he did. Damn it, he did.

Gabe sauntered out and joined the conversation as Clyne wondered again how his neat world had started to spin so badly out of its orbit. Cassidy Walker's arrival in Black Mountain was acting like the impact of a meteor to the surface of the earth. He couldn't breathe past the billowing smoke his grandmother and Gabe were both blowing. He made his excuses and tried for a graceful exit, but his grandmother took a hold of him and extracted a promise that he drive Cassidy to their home.

"She can find it," said Clyne. "She has GPS."

"Which doesn't work half the time out here. You know that. I want you to bring her."

Clyne surrendered and fixed a smile on his face that felt as tight as drying wax. "My pleasure, then, Grandmother."

She patted his cheek, making him feel about six years old and making him flush. He spun and retreated as his grandmother called out a time for him to pick up Agent Walker. He lifted a hand in acknowledgment and escaped to his offices, where he spent much of the afternoon distracted by the clock that ticked down the time until he had to pick up Walker.

As the time approached to head for his home he grew more agitated. Here was another way Agent Walker would know them when he knew little about her. He didn't want to know her or did he?

He wanted his sister back and Cassidy Walker

gone. But Gabe had said that to take a child from her mother was a terrible thing.

Didn't Gabe want his sister home?

At the appointed time, he returned to the police station and Yepa, Gabe's assistant, directed him to the conference room.

"What do you think of her?" asked Yepa.

"I don't think of her."

That made her cock her head and give him a strange look followed by an annoying quirk of her mouth.

Clyne reached the conference room and knocked. Someone called him in and he entered. There they sat, laptops open, files and folders strewn across the table. Juris sat beside Luke, who sat beside Cassidy. To Cassidy's left sat Gabe and beyond him, Sergeant Salvo. Gabe peered over Cassidy's shoulder at her laptop. Clyne narrowed his eyes at the position of Gabe's chair. It seemed far too close to Cassidy. Clyne felt something inside himself growling. Gabe glanced up and his smile of greeting wilted to one of bewilderment. But he moved his chair away from Cassidy, who still stared at her screen.

"You about ready?" asked Clyne.

He noted the change in her body language the instant she heard his voice. Her expression tightened from relaxed to tense and her shoulders stiffened. She did not look at him but closed her laptop and collected her papers, tucking them into a briefcase. She rose and said her farewells. Luke told her he'd see her at Glendora's.

She followed him out, stopping at her car to relieve herself of her briefcase. She carried no purse, which didn't really surprise him, though it was unusual for the women in his acquaintance.

"I'll follow you," she said.

That suited him fine.

"Why did you agree to come?" he asked.

She seemed as if she would not answer. "Curiosity. And my daughter asked me if I've met her brothers. She wants to meet you." It was clear from her tight expression that she did not want this. But he knew that it was only a matter of time. There was no avoiding the inevitable. Jovanna was Indian and so she would be returned to her birth family and tribe.

"And we want to meet her."

Cassidy said nothing to this. She hesitated beside her vehicle.

"How did they get separated, your mother and your sister?"

Clyne drew in a breath and braced to tell the tale as quickly as possible.

"My sister was a very good dancer, jingle and fancy shawl."

She gave him a blank look.

"Those are types of dances. At powwows?"

She nodded half-heartedly.

"There is money in it, if you win. Just like rodeo." Which was how he and then Gabe had made money to help support the family.

"There's a big powwow up in South Dakota on the Sweetgrass reservation. She was bringing Jovanna to her first competition. They got hit head-on by a drunk driver. My mother was killed instantly and Jovanna survived. They were wearing their regalia and my mom's ID was still at the campsite. She was listed as a Jane Doe. It took them a week to even tell us about the accident. By then she was already buried up in the Sweetgrass reservation cemetery."

"But why didn't they ID Jovanna and send her back to you?"

Clyne swiped a hand over his face.

"Because the report said 'no survivors.' We were told she had died with our mom."

"But how?"

"Penmanship. The state police officer wrote one survivor and it got transposed into no survivors on the report."

Cassidy thumped back against the side of her car as she absorbed this.

"How did you figure it out?"

"The cemetery records showed that they buried only one body. We were trying to place a stone lamb on Jovanna's grave and discovered the mistake."

Cassidy swiped a tear from her cheek. Clyne's throat felt tight.

"We better go," he said.

She nodded and slipped into her dark government-issue sedan and started the engine. He trudged to his SUV and led the way. Cassidy followed him in her sedan with the tinted windows. She followed him to the door of his grandmother's home, where she met the first member of their family, Buster, a rather old and partially deaf sheepdog who, at twelve, was the most senior one of them.

The family hound was a mix of several breeds with the long snout of a collie and the mismatched blue and brown eyes of a husky. Buster's legs and face were a buff color and his back showed the blanket common in some collies and shepherd breeds. His full, bushy tail wagged as he reached them.

His walk was stiff but he still bowed a greeting to Cassidy, who offered her hand for Buster's inspection. His white muzzle and clouding eyes revealed his age. Buster was gentle but protective, which was why he was surprised to see him lick Cassidy's hand.

She followed the shepherd mix to the living

room, where his grandmother made introductions to his brothers and their wives and Gabe's fiancé. Uncle Luke arrived for supper. He was wise enough to know that Glendora's cooking was not to be missed. Finally, Cassidy followed him to the table, where they posed for a photo, taken by Luke, and then all sat.

He didn't want her here. So why did he keep looking at her?

His grandmother's table was round so there was no head of the table. But she had placed Cassidy next to him. Better, he thought, for he could keep an eye on her.

In deference to their guest, the family spoke in English. Only the prayer of thanks was offered in Apache. The meal smelled delicious, but the scent of Cassidy kept intruding. She smelled of summer flowers and baby powder and he wanted to tuck her under his arm and inhale.

Cassidy listened as Kino and Clay spoke of their time with the Shadow Wolves on the Arizona border. Gabe relayed tales of when he and Clyne rode the rodeo circuit together. Finally Glendora steered the conversation to Cassidy. She started with Luke, asking how they had met and what it was like working together. Luke's comments were far too glowing for Clyne's taste.

Clyne focused on his meal but his heart

wasn't in it. Cassidy's presence was ruining his appetite.

His grandmother left the table to retrieve the dessert, two fresh-made pecan pies. Kino's wife, Lea, rose heavily to her feet to help serve. Her hand went occasionally to her round belly, caressing the place where her first child grew. Only one more month and Clyne would be an uncle.

Once all the plates were full, Glendora resumed her seat and turned her attention to Cassidy.

"Cassidy, do you have any family out here?" asked Glendora.

Clyne did his best to pretend he wasn't listening.

Cassidy swallowed her mouthful of pie and returned her fork to her plate, correctly judging that the interrogation had finally reached her. "I'm an only child, but both my parents are gone."

"Oh, I'm so sorry. How many brothers and sisters have you, Cassidy?" asked Glendora.

"None."

Glendora blinked as she absorbed this. Clyne knew that his grandmother wanted more children but also had had only one, his mother.

"I see," said his grandmother. "Where's home?"

"I'm an army brat. Moved around a lot. New

England, DC, then up in Alaska for a little while. I also lived in Germany."

"Heavens. A world traveler."

Rootless, thought Clyne. With no home and no people. Only herself and her stolen daughter.

"How did you choose the FBI?" asked Gabe.

Now his brothers were getting into the action. Clyne glanced at his watch, wishing the evening away.

"I enlisted in October of 2001," she said.

Clyne's head jerked up because that was when he had joined the US Marines. Back then he had felt the need to defend his country. Now he only wanted to defend his people and their land.

"I met my husband in basic training. He was deployed before me."

Glendora blinked, her gaze shifting to Cassidy's left hand but their guest wore no ring. Many FBI officers did not.

"You're married?" asked Glendora.

"I was. For seven years. He was a tank commander until he died in Afghanistan in his second deployment, March 4, 2011."

There was a moment of absolute stillness. Cassidy had successfully silenced his grandmother. Clyne did the math and realized Jovanna had been adopted when she was about four and she had been seven when Walker had died. The US tank commander had been her father for only three years. How many occasions had he been home during that time? They would have given him leave, of course. But army tours were two to six years each. Had Walker re-enlisted to support his family?

Cassidy met his gaze with a challenge and held it, those flashing eyes now reminded him of seawater, as blue and deep as the Pacific Ocean. And now he realized what made her different from every other woman he had ever met. She was a warrior and she was a survivor. A veteran who, like him, had lost someone important. Not comrades, though perhaps she had. She had lost her husband.

He looked at her with new eyes, his head cocked as he wondered if he dared to ask if any of the men and women in her unit had been lost.

"He signed for a second tour?" asked Clyne.

"Yes. I stayed home with Amanda and Gerard re-enlisted for another four years. I joined the bureau after my daughter started school. Gerard came home whenever he could."

Clyne's head dropped. He'd made so many assumptions and felt ashamed of himself. He'd even asked her when they had divorced. He rubbed his hand over his forehead and prepared to apologize.

"But I'm not the only veteran at the table. Clyne was in the US Marines. Also enlisted after 9/11. Deployed to Iraq." She turned to him with a sweet smile. "A sharpshooter, right? Thirty-six confirmed kills."

He sucked in a breath. All eyes turned to him as if suddenly he was the stranger at the table. He'd never told them.

Clyne stood and grabbed Cassidy by the arm and hustled her out of the room. She went along but once in the foyer she tugged away, breaking his hold with such ease it startled him into stillness. He'd forgotten that Walker was a fighter, too.

"What's your problem?" she asked.

"I don't talk about that time."

She snorted. "Maybe you should."

He tilted his head to one side, wondering where she got the nerve to tell him what he should do. "What would you know about it?"

"Not much. We were just the ones who had to clean up your mess."

Suddenly he needed to know about her time in the military. Had she seen action?

"Where were you deployed?"

"I flew birds, Black Hawks. Medical transport mostly."

The hairs on his neck lifted again.

"Afghanistan?"

"Iraq, 2003. Don't worry. I didn't transport you. I checked."

So she knew he'd been wounded. He didn't like that she knew so much about him.

How many broken, bleeding bodies had she carried to safety?

"You want me to go back in there?" She glanced toward his waiting family.

He shook his head.

"Call it a night."

She glanced at her watch. "Fine. See you at 0800."

For some reason he wanted to talk to her. Ask her about her tour of duty and maybe learn how she could still carry a gun and enforce the law and fight the bad guys when all he wanted was to stay here where things made sense.

"You know how to find the hotel?" he asked.

"My GPS does. Good night, Cosen," she said. "Please thank your grandmother for the meal. She's an excellent cook."

THE FOLLOWING MORNING, Cassidy left the tribe's casino in the wee hours of the morning, passing through the din of ringing bells and the flash of colored lights that was way too bright for this early in the day. It seemed that most of the guests were white men and women, older, overweight and mesmerized by the whirling wheels and bright digital displays. They sat immobile on the wide stools with coffee and liquor waiting at the ready, their casino players' cards connecting them like umbilical cords to the machines.

Once outside the sun showed no hints of appearance but she paused to savor the clean air. She had spent a lonely night in her vacant hotel room with far too much time to think. Much to her chagrin, her thoughts lingered on Clyne and how he had cared for her when she had been shot. He'd been more than professional; he'd shown a kindness and concern that disquieted. One soldier looking out for another, she told herself. It had to be, because she was not willing to accept that the attraction she battled was mutual.

She reached her vehicle and paused to admire the fine lacy pattern of ice crystals that frosted the windshield. Then she used her gloved hand to scratch an area big enough to peer through. March and still they had frost up here. It was the altitude, she knew, but the terrain was so different from Phoenix. Lovely, really.

She had told Amanda all about her brothers last night. Even sent her the photo that Luke had shared.

Today they would not be investigating Manny Escalanti or searching Salt River for Ronnie Hare because Clyne was heading to Phoenix for another rally against Obella Chemicals. That event would take place at 11 a.m., indoors this time in the civic center. Luke had point, Gabe accompanied Clyne and she had rear security. That meant another three-hour drive by herself behind Clyne's vehicle where her only job was to watch for possible attack from every vehicle they passed. Oh, joy.

At least they had a phone tap on Escalanti. She was considering how to place a camera and microphone in his crib as the procession departed.

Cassidy peered through the gap in the frost as she drove until the defroster softened the edges of the ice, and she attacked the retreating edge with the wiper blades. By the time she reached Black Mountain the window was clear. By the time she reached the Cosen residence, the darkness receded to reveal a gray cloudy morning.

She waited in the drive for the two men. Clyne cast her a glance. He cut a striking figure in his topcoat. She ignored the spark of interest, crushing it out like a cigarette butt.

Luke stopped at her driver's side. "Everything good?"

"All set."

"You got coffee?"

She lifted the paper cup with the casino logo. Luke nodded, grinned and headed to the large SUV that held the tribal seal on the front door.

She pulled out behind them and the small procession started down the mountain. She wished she had her helicopter. Her stomach growled and she fantasized about a piece of Glendora Clawson's pecan pie and the table that had been so full of life and energy. She'd never been at a dinner like that. When she was young she usually ate with her mother. Her father ate on base or after she was in bed. She shifted uncomfortably as she thought of all the dinners that she shared with Amanda over a white pizza box or containers of takeout. The comparison was glaring and not very flattering.

Last night she had met them. The Cosen family. And they were not some terrible monster of clannish bumpkins. They were bright and friendly and connected in ways she could not understand. Being among them made her long for something she had not even known she still wanted. Brothers. Sisters. And the real possibility of nieces and nephews.

Was she wrong to deny her daughter this family? Was she really operating on what was best for Amanda or what was best for Cassidy Marshal Walker?

Gradually the sun emerged; the day brightened and warmed as they wound down the mountain past the rocky outcroppings and red rock.

Cassidy snapped back to focus on the road.

When the dash clock read six forty-five she dialed home and checked in with Amanda, who was using digital flash cards to cram for a science test.

Once she reached Phoenix, Cassidy turned her attention to the event. Another rally. Cosen was an activist of the first order, delivering poignant speeches and garnering support for his causes. They were important causes, she admitted, but her main objective was Cosen's safety, second only to finding something to incriminate him.

They finally reached a two-lane highway and soon afterward arrived at the downtown Phoenix City Center. Then she trailed Luke's vehicle to Phoenix Convention Center and then into the underground parking facility.

She parked in the first available spot, diagonally across from Forrest's vehicle, and climbed stiffly from her sedan. The drive had tightened all her back muscles into one giant ball of muscle spasm. Stretching helped a little.

The air in the parking garage smelled of gasoline, rubber and rotting garbage. The comparison between this and Black Mountain was startling and she began to see what was so appealing.

Agent Forrest and Cosen were out of the SUV

and she headed in their direction as they turned toward the entrance to the convention center.

An engine revved. She caught motion in her peripheral vision. A dark pickup truck took the corner so fast the tires squealed. The truck sped toward them, halogen lights blinding in the subterranean garage. She had time to dive for safety. Instead, she charged forward into Clyne, rushing him out of the way.

"Move," she shouted.

Forrest jumped clear of the front passenger tire. Clyne wrapped an arm about her and together they dove. They landed on the curb. The jolt of pain shot through her healing ribs like a sledgehammer. She caught the blur of a rear tire inches from her face. She grunted and rolled to her back, reaching inside her open blazer for her gun. By the time she scrambled to her feet, Forrest was already up, but the truck had made the turn and disappeared.

"I got a plate," he said.

She turned to Clyne, who lay on his back. He braced himself up on his elbows. His dark trench coat flapped open, revealing the pale denim shirt unbuttoned and, at the throat, a leather cord tied about a small leather pouch. What was that?

"You all right?" she asked.

"Thanks to you, again."

"Who wants you dead, Clyne?" she asked.

"Besides you?" He grinned.

Forrest pulled out his phone. "I'm calling local police." He placed the call and then met Cassidy's gaze. "Almost looked like he was aiming at you, Walker."

"Me?" she asked, her voice filled with disbelief, and then the disbelief ebbed and she fixed her attention on Clyne, who had come to his feet. She scowled at him.

"Did you arrange that?" she asked.

Chapter Eight

Now they were both frowning.

"Me? Why would I do that?"

"Because it's cheaper than paying attorney fees."

"Then the same goes for you, I guess," he said, rolling easily to his feet and standing to dust off his coat.

Cassidy turned to Agent Forrest. "Plate number?"

He lifted the phone from his mouth and gave her the number.

"We get Clyne inside, then I'll run the plate," she said.

Cassidy took Clyne to the security station, such as it was. They at least had offices with good solid doors and locks. Once she had Clyne secured, she began her investigation, calling the office to have them run the plate while Luke coordinated with venue security and the local police on-site. Reinforcements were en route. Registration information was sent to her mobile and showed the vehicle belonged to a member of the Black Mountain tribe.

Cassidy felt him before she saw him and turned to discover Clyne leaning over her shoulder.

"I know him," he said. "Works for the Cattle Association."

"Step back," she ordered.

"I'm not armed."

"I am."

He stepped back.

Forrest joined them. "No sign of the driver yet."

She showed him the registration information and Luke gave a low whistle.

"I'll call Gabe."

The head of the convention center security reported that they had footage of the driver. They all hovered around a large computer screen to watch.

"I know Dale Donner," said Clyne. "He's the tribal livestock manager and would no sooner run me down than run over a child."

"His truck," said Forrest.

"Not the driver. Stake my life on it," said Clyne.

The driver was male but that was about all

they could tell. He wore a ball cap, large sunglasses and possibly a false beard. They printed the images.

"Not him. Too thin," said Clyne.

Over the next hour they made some progress on finding the driver, as the rally participants began to arrive.

Gabe called Clyne to report that Donner was still at home and did not know the truck was missing. Her boss had been notified and he had recommended more agents, a request that Clyne Cosen had quickly declined.

Luke's contact with PPD told them that the police had recovered the truck only three blocks away, illegally parked by a hydrant. Their CSI were processing Donner's truck for latents and physical evidence, which Cassidy knew could take a while. Long enough for the would-be assassin to make another attempt.

It seemed the driver had vanished.

"He followed us all the way from Black Mountain," said Luke.

And she'd never seen him, she realized.

Luke left them to meet with local PD in the hunt for the driver. Phoenix PD was given the description and set out in hopes of getting lucky. Cassidy didn't feel lucky.

Particularly not when she was the one left guarding Clyne Cosen, yet again.

Cassidy turned to Councilman Cosen. She was still unsure if he was the target or if Agent Forrest was correct and the shooter in the truck had been aiming at her. For now, she would act as if Clyne was the objective. But if she could find a connection between him and that driver, it would only strengthen her custody argument.

"You should cancel this appearance," she said.

His answer was immediate. "No."

"Would you consider modifying your schedule? Appearing by video feed?"

"No."

"Canceling the press conference or future outdoor rallies?"

His eye ticked. It was the only evidence she had that he was rattled. "No. Obella Corporation needs to take responsibility for that chemical spill."

"Fine. Send someone else."

"No."

"You are a hard man to keep alive. You realize that?"

He said nothing, just checked the time on his phone. It occurred to her that perhaps Clyne was more interested in causes than breathing. That troubled her.

"You need body armor," she said.

He went pale and wiped his upper lip with the

palm of his hand, rubbing it back and forth over his mouth as if trying to stifle nausea. Finally his hand dropped. But it was shaking.

"No. Not again."

Funny, she thought. Getting shot at and nearly run down had not rattled him. But the mention of body armor made him tremble.

He was a puzzle. Seemingly strong, proud and capable, he had a definite soft spot when it came to his military service. His uncle had mentioned that Clyne used to love to hunt. She wondered if he still did?

"I hear the hunting is great up on Black Mountain," she said.

He eyed her warily, no doubt wondering about the sudden change of topic.

"It is. We have some of the largest elk in the country."

"And guides."

"Yes."

"Would you be willing to guide me?" she asked.

He flinched at the request and turned half-away to collect himself. Then that hand went to his mouth again. He really ought to see someone about this. His behavior had PTSD written all over it. Seeking help was no shame.

She'd taken advantage of a grief counselor after Gerard had died. It had helped. But

Amanda had helped more. Her daughter gave her a reason to get up and make breakfast and go outside and reengage with the world. Eventually the joy had returned. What would happen if she lost Amanda?

"I don't guide," said Clyne, now apparently recovered. "But Clay is an excellent guide. I'm sure you would have some luck."

She nodded her head and smiled. It was good to know your enemy's weakness.

His eyes narrowed right back.

"Have you ever killed a man, Cassidy?"

That question did not come out of the blue. He was probing her weaknesses, just as she had done to him. Still, she didn't entirely keep herself from reacting. Her heart rate increased as she sucked in a breath. She held it and then let go in a long easy release. She wasn't going to let this particular man rattle her.

Cassidy knew this was the sharpshooter speaking. Seeking another connection with her that transcended the physical.

"Have you, Cassidy? Have you looked down your sights and taken his life? Stolen him from his family and from all future generations?"

She had. Twice. Cassidy looked at Clyne.

Thirty-six confirmed kills.

"I took down an armed bank robber in Phoenix. The guy had hit over eleven banks. And when we got to number twelve, he had hostages. I didn't feel bad about it. Not even afterward. I wasn't the only one who shot him, but it was my bullet that killed him. At least that's what the ME said. There was also a kidnapper in Chandler." She glanced away, swallowing down the gall rising in her throat. She stopped talking as her stomach tensed. She remembered him, Brett Parker, the man who had snatched a toddler right out of the child's bedroom window. A few days later, she'd been there to take him down. The arrest went bad. He had killed the child almost immediately. Never meant to ransom her. Now she carried the memory of that dead girl and also her finger on the trigger when she sighted Parker. She remembered the recoil of her gun, the training that included everything but how to watch a man you killed die before your eyes. That moment entangled with the discovery of the child, submerged in that stream. They lived in her mind, repeating like a spliced video loop until she'd come to accept that she would never forget them, either of them, killer and victim. Wolf and lamb. Couldn't. It was emblazoned on her memory, etched like the bullet from the barrel of her gun. She glanced at Clyne, met his steady gaze. Thirty-six kills. Thirty-six memories he could never erase. She scrubbed her hands over her face and shook off the horror.

"It was unavoidable," she said, her voice straining. "And he can't hurt anyone again."

"Because you stopped him."

As he had stopped thirty-six. Had any of them been women or children? She couldn't ask.

"Yes," she whispered. "I stopped him." She met his gaze, seeing the dangerous glitter in the eyes of a dangerous man.

"You should cancel your speech."

Clyne's face showed nothing but determination.

"Not a chance."

Cassidy was relieved to see the reinforcements from her department arrive. Security was tight for the rally and Clyne, minus his body armor, spoke to a crowd of energetic activists. She was so busy watching for threats that she almost did not hear his speech. But his rich baritone did break her concentration, rumbling through her like a far-off locomotive.

After the rally, Clyne met with local officials, was interviewed by the media and finally headed back to security, where he could not be convinced to allow additional agents onto his sacred land. So it was Cassidy and Luke again, winding back up the mountain at midday. Gabe met them at the border of the reservation with another officer, who escorted them to tribal headquarters. Luke left them there and she followed Clyne back to his offices, where it seemed the entire tribal council and half the police force waited to greet them.

She filled Gabe in on everything that had happened while Clyne busied himself with his computer.

Both their phones awoke simultaneously, hers beeping and his pounding some tribal drum ring tone. She retrieved hers first and saw the name and image of her attorney appear on the screen. Her jaw dropped and she glanced to Clyne. He was scowling at his phone and then his eyes met hers.

His attorney. She was certain.

They both held their ringing phones in statuesque silence for one more instant. It could mean only one thing. The judge had made a ruling on her appeal.

They both turned, giving each other their backs as they took the calls.

Cassidy punched the answer button.

"Hello?"

Chapter Nine

Her attorney continued as Cassidy tried to understand what he was saying.

"But she's twelve," said Cassidy. "By law, Amanda is old enough to choose to be adopted outside her tribe."

Her attorney's breath rattled across his phone's mic sounding to her like static. "The judge felt it was not a fair choice for Amanda to make since she does not remember her family."

"*I'm* her family," Cassidy snarled into the phone. Why did this have to happen in the center of tribal headquarters, in front of half his tribe?

"I'm sorry, Cassidy. Child Protective Services is on their way now to pick her up."

"Now?"

Cassidy was on her feet. She didn't remember clearing the doorway or leaving her assignment.

She just found herself in the parking area, rummaging for her keys as she clutched the phone to her ear.

"I'm coming."

"No. Don't," her attorney said.

"But they can't just take her," she said.

"They *are* taking her. I'll head over there now. But I can't stop them."

"How long?" she asked.

"Six months," he said.

She sucked in a breath.

"Can I go with her? Help her with the transition?"

"No."

She'd see about that.

"I have to go." She hung up and then fumbled to pull up her contact favorites list on her mobile but her fingers weren't working right and the screen blurred. She swore and tried again.

Amanda was at school, of course, and could not pick up. Her daughter was allowed to carry her phone but could use it only at lunch and before and after school.

Cassidy was calling Gerard's mother when she received a text reply from Amanda. The phone began to ring as Amanda's message popped up.

?up

Cassidy translated her daughter's message. *What's up?*

Gerard's mother answered. Cassidy's voice cracked as she rushed to tell Diane the situation.

"Should I go to the school?"

Cassidy didn't know. Diane couldn't stop them from taking her granddaughter, but she could speak to Amanda first.

Amanda's next message popped up.

mom u there? w/b

Cassidy translated her daughter's message. *Mom? Are you there? Write back.*

"Yes. Please tell her."

"Can she come back here, pack some clothing?"

"I don't know. Bring her some things. But hurry. Diane. Hurry. They'll be there soon."

She disconnected and saw Clyne alone in the lot, heading her way with his phone glued to his ear. He didn't have the look of triumph she had expected. Why hadn't she anticipated that when they served the judge Amanda's notarized request that something like this could happen?

The Indian Child Welfare Act was very clear.

There were only three reasons a Native American child could be adopted outside their tribe. If the adopting parent was the biological parent. If no member of the child's tribe was willing to adopt and finally, if the child had attained the age of twelve years and chose to be adopted outside the tribe. It was this final stipulation that Cassidy's attorney had argued. And received a conditional denial because Amanda had been only two when she left her birth family.

Cassidy had been aware of the ICWA when she adopted Amanda but as her daughter had no kin, the issue seemed moot. During this challenge, her attorney had been so certain that, regardless of the ruling, Amanda, since she was now twelve, could just choose to be adopted away from the Cosens.

If she'd had even an inkling this might happen, she would have been home guarding her daughter instead of up here on Black Mountain.

What was a conditional denial anyway?

Cassidy didn't know what kept her upright. The pain in her chest was swelling like a balloon. She could hardly breathe. She tried to text but her fingers, clumsy on the tiny keyboard, made a mess. She swiped at the tears and checked Clyne's progress. She had to get a message to Amanda.

thr comeing. Judge rules U going 2 biological family 6 mo. today.

Clyne reached her. She turned away, clinging to her phone. Her lifeline to her daughter.

WDYS? Mom? WDYM? ?U@

Cassidy interpreted her daughter's text. *What did you say, Mom? What did you mean? Where are you?*

Cassidy tried again, typing madly. Wishing she had learned more slang so she could write faster. Her phone dinged again.

cnt tx. po po <3 u. *4

Cassidy read the message. *Can't text. Police. Love you. Kiss for...*

*4U. Kiss for...*you.* It was how Amanda ended all her texts. But her daughter had not had time to finish. They had her phone. They had her. Cassidy burst into tears.

Clyne touched her shoulder. "Cassidy, I'm sorry."

She didn't resist as he dragged her in and held her right there before the tribe members streaming by on the way to headquarters. She should pull away and tell him she didn't need his sympathy. Instead she clung and sobbed.

"They're taking her."

"I know."

"I'm not there with her."

"It will be all right."

She clung, burying her face in his topcoat, smelling wool and the faint aroma of cedar and sage, and gave voice to her deepest fear.

"Six months!" she sobbed.

Clyne stroked her head. "Come on. We have to go back in."

She pushed back. "No. I can't."

"All right, Cassidy." He glanced back toward the tribal headquarters and his brother Gabe. "Let me get you away from here."

She let him guide her to the passenger side of her sedan. She slipped into the seat and he closed the door. Clyne took the driver's side and asked for her keys. She pressed them into his palm.

"They have her," she said, her voice just a whisper.

"I know."

"Will you let me see her, just for a minute, to explain?"

Clyne gave her a look of pity. He'd won. He could afford to be gracious or not. By the time she had her tears reined in, she realized they were pulling into the casino hotel. Clyne guided her through the lobby. She should be looking for threats, but she ducked her head, like a coward and allowed him to lead her along. Even after Gerard's passing, she had never felt so lost.

Of course Clyne knew everyone at reception and several of the folks working the floor. Even in the elevator he met an acquaintance. She was happy her dark glasses covered her eyes but knew they didn't mask the tears running down her cheeks or the pink nose that always accompanied her waterworks. She hadn't cried since Gerard's funeral and then only after his family had departed, Amanda had retired and she was alone in her bedroom.

Clyne helped her with her key card. She remembered to lock the door behind them and throw the latch.

He said nothing to this precaution as they made their way into the room. He crossed to the window and drew back the curtains. She sank into the love seat.

"Got a view of the mountain," he said. "That mountain is sacred to us. We believe that we are related to the stone, trees and wind. The mountain is a relative and there are spirits that live there. They are called Ga'an."

She cradled her head in her hands, trying to stop her shoulders from shuddering as she listened to the soft melody of his voice telling her the origin of his people.

He sat on the long rectangular footstool, his legs splayed on either side of hers. He rested a hand lightly on her knee.

"In our ceremonies, Apache men dress as the Ga'an, Crown Dancers, summoning the mountain spirits to help protect our people from disease and evil. I have been a Crown Dancer. All my brothers have been. Together we have danced for our people. There are five spirits, four Crown dancers who are painted all in white and one sacred clown in black. During the dance, they *are* the spirits. Their dance protects the tribe. Perhaps you have seen photos of men in masks with large wooden headdresses?"

She shrugged, thinking she had not.

"Well, that is the embodiment of the Ga'an. The headdresses are made by powerful medicine men and blessed in a sacred ceremony. When the Ga'an dance together, they are powerful. But more powerful still is Changing Woman. She is a goddess who makes the land and people fruitful. Every spring she is young. In the summer she is fertile. In the fall she is bountiful and in winter, she grows old. But come spring she is young again. Once she grew so lonely that she made man and woman out of a piece of her own skin."

Cassidy lowered her hands from her eyes, mesmerized by his voice as much as his words.

"When a child is born, Changing Woman will dance. She is also called White Painted Woman. We have ceremonies for births, weddings and to bless a home. She also dances at the coming of age ceremony for girls. It is like a sweet-sixteen party, wedding and New Year's festival all mixed together. But also like a christening, because it is when a girl is welcomed to the tribe as an adult. The ceremony takes four days."

"Four?"

"Yes. Much of this time the girl must dance. Apache girls must prove they are strong enough to be Apache women. Part of the ceremony involves painting the child white. By doing so, she becomes the embodiment of Changing Woman. Her dance is sacred. All girls look forward to their Sunrise Ceremony."

Cassidy's suspicions stirred. "You didn't tell me this to distract me."

"No. I did not."

"Why, then?" But she was certain she already knew.

"My brothers and I have dreamed of dancing at our sister's Sunrise Ceremony. My grandmother has made her dress and moccasins."

"When does a girl become a woman?"

"In the summer she turns thirteen."

"Amanda is only twelve and a half."

Clyne shook his head. "She will be thirteen this summer. The ceremony takes place on July 4 each year. It will be good for this to be a day of celebration."

And they would still have her then. She could become Changing Woman and afterward she would be an Apache woman. And then, she would have to choose between the family of her birth and the one she had made that day when she took Gerard's hand.

Cassidy stood and excused herself to wash her face and repair her hair. She gave up on her hair and left it down. Another month's growth and she could resume her low ponytail.

She found Clyne standing by the window. She slowed, hesitated and considered retreat. He turned to her and smiled. The upturning of his mouth transformed his face from statuesque beauty to a man with more sex appeal than any one person should possess.

"There is so much I need to tell you about her." She came to stand beside him. "She is allergic to kiwis and she hates spiders. She loves animals. Always wanted a dog. She loves sports and she is a really good skier. Surfer, too, but I can't see…"

He pressed a finger to her lips. She was babbling.

"She's our sister. We will take care of her." His finger slipped over her bottom lip and away, leaving a soft sexual tingle in its wake.

She looked up at him. He nodded.

"We will."

She let her shoulders sag and accepted what she could not change.

"All right, then."

They stared for a moment and her skin began that tingling itch, an awareness that did not need touch to come alive. Just to be near him made her entire body quicken.

"I really wanted to hate you," she whispered.

"Don't you?"

She shook her head. "I think your family is wonderful and that Amanda will be very lucky to have you all as brothers."

She didn't say the rest aloud. Amanda would have the big family she had always wanted, the kind of family Cassidy had once fantasized of having when she was a lonely little girl moving with her parents from base to base.

"I'm not giving up. I still want her to pick me."

His mouth quirked. "Of course."

He stepped closer, lifting his hands and gently held her at the shoulders. He pressed his lips together as if trying to keep himself from speaking. Bit by bit his mouth relaxed into the full sensual wonder it was.

"I think she is very lucky to have a mother like you. Strong, capable and it's clear you love your daughter."

She lifted her brows, half expecting him to qualify his words. He didn't. Instead he used a crooked index finger to lift her chin. His gaze dipped to her mouth and she knew he was going to kiss her.

Oh, no, no, no, cried her mind. *Yes,* whispered her heart.

Cassidy rocked forward, moving to meet the soft brushing of lips. It was just a whisper of a kiss yet it dropped inside her like the first domino to fall, sending the rest toppling in turn. Her arms went about his neck, keeping him from escape as she lifted to her toes and rocked closer, taking his mouth against hers.

It had been so long. So damned long and she never ever thought to find this kind of electricity, had never expected it to strike twice.

His hands splayed across her back. One high and one low at that place where her back became her backside. He pressed and she yielded, letting her hips drop against his and finding what she had expected, hard male flesh. She wanted this, wanted him. And there was no doubt that he wanted her.

Chapter Ten

Clyne had only meant to comfort her. But deep down, underneath his compassion, something stirred. Something dangerous.

Clyne breathed in as the sweet fragrance of coconut and hibiscus rose to greet him. Walker smelled more like Hawaii than Arizona.

He drew back to look at her and immediately recognized another mistake. She was captivating. Her fine hair now brushed her shoulders, accentuating her beauty. Her face was heart-shaped and her cheeks and lips a becoming pink. She wore tiny diamond studs on her earlobes. They flashed when she moved and drew attention to the graceful curve of her neck. Field Agent Walker had a lovely complexion. Pale, but lovely.

She was a head shorter than he was and her build was slim and athletic. Clyne preferred more curves and a darker complexion. He'd dated a few white women, but never for long and never a blonde. Yet here he was, alone in her room, thinking of what she would taste like.

No. He should walk away. But he didn't.

If he could just figure out what the attraction was, perhaps he could stop it or kill it. Because he was not getting tangled up in a relationship with Cassidy Walker.

She'd been married. She carried a gun. She was a federal officer. And she had adopted his sister. Any one of those made good cause for him to stay the heck away from her.

"We shouldn't," he said.

She stiffened and her fingers, laced behind his neck, slipped to his shoulders, then dropped away.

"It's a huge mistake. I don't want this," she said.

"Neither do I."

He stared at her Pacific-blue eyes and knew he was a liar. He wanted her. He just didn't want what came along with her. A white woman. It wasn't in the plan. He was going to marry a woman who shared his culture and his heritage. This woman was a complication—a trap.

"You and I, you're an assignment. I'll be gone in a few weeks."

"Yes. I know." But instead of being a reason to step away, her words gave urgency to his desire. They lacked the luxury of time and the knowledge that it could not last made the connection even more tempting.

She stepped back and away, facing the windows. Clyne eyed her and knew that whatever was between them, words and distance would not staunch. Would bedding her put this behind them both or would it only open the floodgates wider?

He was usually wise. He was usually cautious. Usually.

Clyne advanced. Cassidy lifted her phone.

"I have to check in."

He smiled. "Yes. Me, too."

She called his uncle and Clyne realized that Luke likely knew a great deal about Cassidy. They had worked together on several assignments.

Cassidy's conversation broke into his musings.

"Where?" she asked and there was a pause. "You want me along?" Another pause. "All right. I understand. I'll go over the audio here. Yes, I'll do that. Call if you find him." She tucked away the phone.

Clyne asked the question without words.

She made a face, clearly not inclined to tell him the subject of her business.

"Luke has a lead on Ronnie Hare."

Ronnie Hare was the parole officer who had been running messages from the cartels to the Wolf Posse. Gabe had nearly caught him in January, but he had escaped.

"That's good," said Clyne.

"Yeah. His cooperation would help us make a case against Escalanti, for sure. The police on Salt River Reservation had his family under surveillance but there has been nothing. So we suggested watching a few of his parolees. We got a possible hit."

"You going?"

"Tomorrow, maybe. I was hoping…"

He didn't jump to her rescue but made her ask him.

"I'd like to see Amanda."

Clyne considered the wisdom of having the girl's adoptive mother there when she arrived.

"No."

She looked as if he had punched her in the face.

"What if she's frightened?"

"Jovanna is my sister. I'll protect her with my life."

"I'm not talking about protection. I'm talking about a child being taken from everything that is familiar."

"She's Apache. She's strong."

"She's a little girl whose favorite color is still pink."

Clyne set his jaw and hardened his heart to her pleas.

Cassidy threw up a hand, stormed away, spun and retraced her steps. Then she folded her arms before her, jutted one hip and worked a brow.

"Do you know what music she likes to listen to when she's going to sleep? Or her favorite foods or the names of her closest friends?"

He didn't, of course. "Those things will come once she takes her place in her family."

Cassidy's jaw twitched. "She's not a clock for your mantel. She's a little girl who still leaves a tooth under her pillow for the tooth fairy."

Clyne remained unyielding, though the doubt cramped his belly. What if she was unwilling to know them? Angry at being forced from the home of this fierce little woman?

"I will bring you to see her. But only if she is not aware of your presence."

TWO HOURS LATER Clyne sat in the darkness in his SUV beside Cassidy Walker. The two floodlights in his grandmother's driveway illuminated the yard and road beyond. Glendora Clawson and her husband, Hex, had not waited for Housing and Urban Development to assign them a residence like many on the rez.

Instead they'd built a four-bedroom home that had been larger than they needed to raise their only daughter, his mother, Tessa.

His phone rang and he took the call from Gabe. Cassidy watched him as if she were on surveillance until he hung up.

"They reached Black Mountain. She should be here any minute."

Cassidy directed her attention to the road. A few minutes later a string of three cars turned in. Kino led the procession in his tribal police cruiser. Next came the dark Ford sedan from Child Protective Services and Gabe had the tail in his white SUV.

Cassidy leaned forward as doors opened and the two Cosen brothers appeared. Next came a woman from the rear seat of the Ford. She wore a green down coat that made her look like a walking sleeping bag. The driver emerged, a white man in a black woolen topcoat and red scarf. Finally he could see his sister.

Jovanna slipped from the backseat and into the circle illuminated by the floodlights. She wore a pink nylon jacket unzipped and the floppy sheepskin boots popular with young girls. Her face reminded him of his mother's in the photos of Tessa as a girl. Only the smile was missing. She had wide brown eyes and a soft round face. Her dark hair had been dyed blond at the tips and strands hung over her face like a shield.

"She's here," said Cassidy and reached for the door, before remembering that she was to stay in the car. She sunk back into the seat, then rebounded to lean so far forward that her forehead struck the window.

His grandmother was out of the house now, flying down the stairs, her arms flung wide. Jovanna had time to straighten before Glendora had her in her arms. Clyne smiled as Amanda all but disappeared in the bear hug. His grandmother was weeping, of course. Jovanna's hands came up and she wrapped her arms about her grandmother. Glendora tucked her grandchild under one arm and motioned to her grandsons. Gabe came forward, Stetson in hand, and leaned to touch his forehead to his sister's. Kino repeated the greeting and then gave Jovanna a hug.

Jovanna, now sandwiched between his youngest brother and his grandmother, was ushered toward the door, where Kino's wife, Lea, stood with a hand on her protruding belly beside Clay's wife, Isabella. Clay stepped from the house holding the collar of a large sheepdog.

Buster she remembered. The dog strained and jumped to be free of Clay's grip. Clay released the shepherd, who flew down the steps and right to Jovanna. His sister took a step back and lifted her hands to ward off attack but Buster threw himself to the ground, rolling and kicking like a submissive puppy. Then he sprang to his feet and tore away and back to Jovanna before throwing himself down again.

Clyne felt a catch in his throat. Buster remembered the lost member of their family. Jovanna knelt beside their family pet and buried her face in the warm coat.

"She always wanted a dog. Talked about a big shaggy dog. How old is Buster?"

Clyne found his voice held a telling quaver when he spoke. "He's twelve."

Jovanna's face now received a thorough licking as she laughed and straightened. Clay stepped forward to greet Jovanna by touching foreheads and his sister seemed to already have adjusted to this traditional form of greeting.

Clay introduced his wife and then his sister-in-law. Clyne now wondered why he had agreed to bring Cassidy. He was not there to greet his sister as he should be and Cassidy did not seem comforted judging from the tears now streaming down her face.

"She looks like them. Like all of you." Cassidy's words were choked with emotion.

"She looks like our mother," he said. "Her name was Tessa."

The door opened and the gathering filed inside, Buster sticking to Jovanna's side as she crossed the threshold. Gabe glanced toward Clyne's SUV and nodded before closing the door.

Clyne started the engine and drove Cassidy back to her hotel. Right now Glendora would be showing Jovanna the room they had repurposed for her with the blanket that had once graced his mother's bed.

Cassidy was silent during the drive except for an occasional choking sound. Clyne did not like to see a woman in pain even if it was the woman he had fought in court for the past eight months.

"I'm sorry," he said. "My family owes you a great debt."

That seemed to stiffen her spine. "Don't you dare thank me. I haven't lost her yet."

Once at the casino entrance he tried to walk her in but she stopped him with an outstretched hand.

"Leave me be, Clyne."

He watched her walk away and wondered why he felt compelled to follow her rather than return to his family. She was messing with his head and making him question what he knew to be true. Jovanna belonged with her tribe and her family. And Cassidy was once a soldier. Surely she understood collateral damage.

Clyne forced himself back into his car. Jovanna was home, where she belonged. He'd won. So why did his chest hurt?

Chapter Eleven

When Clyne arrived home, the late supper was nearly ready and he could not understand why he did not feel the satisfaction he had expected to experience at this moment.

Glendora ushered Jovanna over to him and he looked down at the girl he had dreamed of since he'd learned she survived. He compared her against the little child she had been. He had not been there when she was born because he'd been on a rooftop in Iraq. And on the day his sister had left them for her first competition in South Dakota, he'd been riding the rodeo and sending all he could from his winnings back to his mom, who had just separated from their dad. He had seen his sister briefly, then almost two, on visits home. Kino, the youngest of the brothers, had been nine when Jovanna was born.

Jovanna stood and accepted the touching of foreheads and then the greeting in Apache that she did not return. The spark of fury ignited. She'd been robbed of her native tongue, her culture and her family. All because of a stupid bureaucratic mistake. If not for that mistake Cassidy would have a Sioux baby who had no other home and his family would never have lost Jovanna. But then he would never have known Cassidy.

That didn't matter. It couldn't.

"Jovanna, do you remember me?" Clyne asked.

She gave her head a little shake and her silky hair slipped over her shoulders. He stared at the blond tips that he now saw had a distinctive pink tint.

He lifted a strand and scowled at the cultural intrusion. This little girl was now as much white as she was Apache.

"Well, perhaps in time," he said and released her hair. "We welcome you back to your home. Our people have lived in this place for thousands of years."

She looked around and then back to him. "Doesn't seem big enough for all those people."

Kino burst out laughing. Jovanna had a sense of humor. He quirked a brow not sure if that was good or bad.

"Supper time," announced Glendora.

Jovanna rested a hand on Buster, who accompanied her to the table and sat at her feet. It seemed this shepherd was not going to let this sheep out of his sight again. He looked at Clay with his bicolored eyes as if to say, "You lost her."

It was only an ordinary Wednesday but his grandmother had made it a holiday with a pot roast cooked with potatoes and root vegetables. Nothing too exotic. But when they sat to eat, after the prayer to thank the food, Clyne noted that Jovanna did not take any of the meat.

Glendora noted the same thing and glanced to him in confusion. His sister's plate consisted of bread and green beans.

"Is there something wrong?" asked Glendora.

"Um. No, everything is fine," said Jovanna, looking very small surrounded by her brothers and their wives.

"You don't like pot roast or potatoes?"

"I love potatoes. It's just…"

Lea took up the conversation. "I couldn't eat meat when I first got pregnant. Just the smell." She rolled her eyes.

Clay looked at Jovanna and hazarded a guess. "You're a vegetarian?"

Jovanna nodded. "Yes."

"What? You're Apache. We've raised cattle for hundreds of years. We all have cattle in the communal herd. This is from our herd," he said motioning toward the meat.

"I don't eat anything with a face," she said, but her voice now trembled.

Glendora placed a hand on Clyne's arm, a signal to stop talking.

"The potatoes don't have a face, unless you count the eyes."

Jovanna smiled. "But they were cooked with the meat. I'm sorry, Grandmother. I don't want to be rude. I just think animals should not be food."

"That's ridiculous," said Clyne.

Jovanna's eyes went wide and glassy.

His grandmother rose from the table and disappeared into the kitchen.

"We're hunters and ranchers," said Clyne, lifting his hands in frustration. "We have some of the best trout fishing in the country not twenty minutes from here." He pointed east toward Pinyon Lake.

Jovanna seemed to grow smaller in her seat.

His grandmother returned with a jar of peanut butter and jelly.

Jovanna smiled as a look of relief lifted her features.

Clyne's scowl deepened. Peanut butter and jelly, on the dinner table.

He continued to glower as Kino took up the

conversation, recalling tales of his childhood of which Clyne had no recollection because he had already been in the service at that time. Kino told stories that involved Jovanna. When he mentioned the time she had used a green marker to color the family dog and herself, Jovanna straightened.

"I remember that!" She looked at her hands as if seeing the green marks. "I remember that. How old was I?"

Kino's smile was sad. "You just turned two. It was right before the contest. Mom was furious because she didn't think the ink would come off before then."

Clay broke in. "I was supposed to be watching you, so it was my fault. Boy, was she angry." He smiled.

"She scrubbed me in the tub." Jovanna pointed to the bathroom. "Here. In this house." And she inhaled and looked around as if for the first time. "I lived here!"

"That's right," said Glendora. She expertly made a peanut butter and jelly sandwich and offered it to Jovanna.

"Why did we live with you, Grandma?"

The men went quiet but Glendora replied. "Your mom and dad were having some trouble."

Some trouble, thought Clyne. His dad had been a drug trafficker and his mom had been right to get his siblings clear of him. It was what Clyne had used his signing bonus on. Money for his mother and siblings until she could get her feet under her.

"Where is he?" she asked.

Kino went pale. He'd been there, hiding under a kitchen table in their dad's home when their father's contact had murdered their dad. Thankfully a tablecloth had kept him from seeing Kino but also kept his little brother from seeing the killer's face.

"He's gone, too, sweetie," said Glendora. "He died a long time ago."

"Oh," said Jovanna, and her expression of joy dropped.

His sister would never know their father. Clyne didn't know if he should be heartbroken or relieved. Both, he decided.

The somber moment passed when Clay launched into stories of their mother. How she sewed contest regalia for powwow dance competitions and danced. Jovanna munched her peanut butter sandwich and drank her milk. After the meal they shared a cake with Welcome Home Jovanna written in blue frosting on the top.

Everything went well until Kino and Clay said good-night and left with their wives. Gabe announced the ongoing investigation and took his leave shortly afterward. His grandmother took Jovanna down the hall to the bedroom and he and Buster trailed along. His sister had only her school backpack, so Glendora offered a worn flannel nightie that looked miles too big for her granddaughter. On the bed, Glendora had placed some of the stuffed animals that had belonged to Jovanna a lifetime ago. Buster left Clyne's side to sit at Jovanna's bedside, resting his head on her knee.

Jovanna sat on the bed and lifted a lavender elephant with wide felt eyes. She studied the toy she once called Fafa and tucked it under her arm. Then she set it aside and rested a hand on Buster's head.

"Do you have a Wi-Fi code?" asked Jovanna.

"A what?" asked Glendora.

"To connect to the internet. I want to write my mom."

Glendora glanced to him. He shook his head.

"I'm sorry, sweetheart. We don't have that here."

"Oh." Jovanna did not quite hide the crest-fallen look.

From there it all fell apart. It must have struck her that she was going to spend the night in a strange house with these strangers who were her family.

Her lip trembled and tears sprang from her

eyes. She sank to the floor and wrapped her arms about Buster. Her words where more wail than speech.

"I want my mom!"

Glendora spent the next hour trying to comfort Jovanna while Clyne paced up and down in the hallway.

In his mind, Jovanna's return had gone much differently. Jovanna would remember them and slip back into her old life. Now he saw the problem with that plan. He'd never really considered his sister's feelings. Only what was best for her.

Gabe had tried to warn him. Even said flat out that their sister had already lost one mother and that making her lose another would be cruel.

Cruel.

That was something Clyne never intended. He knew it was best for children to be raised by their tribe. He knew in his heart that without that heritage the Indian part of them died. But his philosophical and moral stand did not take into consideration the pain of his sister's tears.

Her first night back with her family and Jovanna was sobbing into Buster's damp fur.

Glendora stepped out into the hall. She held the doorknob as she met Clyne's gaze.

"What do we do?"

"Only thing to do is let her cry. She's homesick."

"But this is her home," said Clyne.

"She's not a cactus. You can't just plop her down anywhere and expect her to grow."

"She belongs here."

"She does. But she was just escorted from her school by police officers and dropped here like a sack of laundry. She wants to be a part of this family and to have her big brothers around her. But Clay and Kino won't be here for her. They're starting families of their own. Gabe is going to marry Selena.

Which was a mistake. He'd already told Gabe that Selena's connections to illegal doings would be nothing but a problem to him and his reputation.

"Where is Agent Walker staying?" asked Glendora.

Clyne's heart sank.

"The casino hotel. Why?"

"Maybe she could come by. Tuck in her little girl."

"That's a bad idea."

"Why?"

"Because we won custody but only for six months. Then Jovanna will have to choose. If I let Walker in here, she might pick her."

"You're thinking what to do in six months."

Glendora inclined her head toward the door and the sobbing that came from within. "I am thinking of a little girl missing her mother."

"She is not her mother."

Glendora looked ready to cry herself. Her daughter, his mother, had lost her life and her chance to raise her baby girl.

Clyne dragged in a long breath and let it go. "I'll go get her."

Glendora turned the knob and reentered the room, leaving the door ajar.

"Honey Bear, your brother is going to fetch your mama."

Jovanna's face came up from her pillow and stared at Clyne. Then she lifted the dragging hem of her nightgown and rushed to him, wrapping her arms about his middle and clinging like a monkey.

"Thank you, Clyne. *Ixehe.*"

Clyne stroked Jovanna's hair. His sister had just thanked him in Apache. Did she recall the language of her birth or had she learned it before returning to them?

He looked to Glendora, who was crying now. He just knew he was going to regret this. But he whispered to his sister in Apache that he would take care of her and that everything would be all right.

Chapter Twelve

Cassidy had just finished a call with Luke. They'd successfully followed one of the Salt River gang members to a remote location where he had left food and supplies at a drop. They were feeding someone and he believed it was Hare. He was staying on surveillance for the night.

"I have the calls from Escalanti," she said.

"Anything good?"

"I don't know. The tech guys couldn't provide transcripts. It's all Apache."

Luke made a sound in his throat. "Gabe, Kino or Clyne can translate. Clay, too. Any of them."

Like she'd ask them.

When she didn't respond Luke spoke again.

"Cassidy. Don't be stubborn. There might be something there. Get it translated."

"I will," she promised.

Luke said good-night and she ended the call.

She was heading for the shower, dressed only in her underwear when the knock sounded on her door. A firm rapping, unlike the polite tentative rap of housekeeping.

Cassidy stepped into the bathroom to retrieve her pistol. She wasn't going to stand in front of that peephole and ask who was there after the two attacks.

"Who is it?" she called from the security of the bathroom.

"Clyne Cosen."

She lowered the pistol. Cosen? At this hour. Her suspicions peaked. Had he come to finish what they'd started? Her body came alive, tingling all over. That made her scowl. His timing sucked. She'd just finished up another round of tears before Luke phoned.

The nerve of hitting on her when he knew she would be sad and vulnerable. What a jerk.

"I'm not that lonely."

"Open the door, Cassidy. Jovanna needs you."

She shoved the pistol into her holster as she left the bathroom, and threw back the metal latch, released the lock and tugged open the door. The breeze from the hallway reminded her that she was wearing only a fuchsia lace bra and matching panties.

Clyne's eyes widened as he swept down the length of her, reversed course and lingered at the swell of her breasts. The lace cups of her bra did not include a lining, and she felt her nipples pucker up under the contact of nothing more than his stare.

When he finally met her gaze his eyes were glittering with an unmistakable intensity that had her backing up. Her ears tingled with the rest of her.

"Lace?" he said.

Cassidy ducked into the bathroom and grabbed a white bath towel winding it around herself. It covered her from beneath her armpits to just below her hips.

Her throat had gone dry and a glance in the mirror showed her that her skin was flushed nearly as pink as her underthings.

"I was about to take a shower," she said.

Clyne remained in the hallway as if refusing to take the step that would lead him again over her threshold.

"Yes, I see."

He certainly had.

"You said Amanda needs me?" He'd actually said Jovanna. But she refused to speak that name. The only person who could make her say otherwise was her daughter.

"She's crying. My grandmother sent me to fetch you."

Cassidy let the towel drop as she rushed back

into the room to retrieve her trousers. She slipped into her blouse and fumbled with the buttons, noticed they were out of alignment and left them that way as she reached for her coat. By the time she had her boots on and holster clipped Clyne was using a bandanna to wipe his brow.

"Hot?" she said with a wicked smile. The temperature in the hall was anything but. March up in the mountains felt more like January to her.

"Yeah," he said, casting her a doleful look. "Ready?"

Cassidy slipped her phone into her pocket with the charger and scooped up her computer. Everything else she could live without.

He walked with her through the casino, greeting various members of his circle as he escorted her out and to the large SUV.

"Should I follow you?"

"I'll drive you back." Her radar went up again as she imagined Clyne walking her to her room late at night, lingering outside her door with that big empty bed inside.

"I'll take my car."

"Fine."

He drove her to the lot, following her directions. When she told him to stop, he did and then turned to her.

"Did you really think that I'd come back for…"

She closed the door because she was sick of him seeing her turn pink every time he asked her a question.

"Listen, I'm sorry about that."

"Would you have let me in, Cassidy, if I had been there for that?"

"What do you think?" She tried for a look of impatience but her stomach was tightening and her toes curled in her boots as she looked at his appealing features and that wide, full mouth. Her mind flashed an image of that mouth fixed on her breast, his tongue working against the lace cup of her bra.

His mouth quirked and she lifted her gaze to meet his. His eyes held the glitter of desire that fueled her own.

"Let's go," she said and pulled the latch before slipping out into the crisp evening air. She was afraid cold air would not be enough to cool her heated blood but she kept walking.

CLYNE STOOD LIKE a silent sentinel as Cassidy spoke with her daughter. Their reunion had tugged at his heart and made him question his decisions to end her custody.

It was clear that Cassidy loved Jovanna and that Jovanna adored her mom. He considered for the first time that Jovanna would not choose to remain with her brothers after the six months were over. Even his grandmother didn't think Jovanna would pick them. She might learn to love them, but she already loved Cassidy Walker.

Now Clyne had to think of a way to keep Jovanna here, even if his sister chose Walker. His gaze flicked to the woman in question. There was no doubt what she wanted. She had told him. She was going to get her promotion and move east. She was going to take Jovanna. He had to think of a way to stop her.

Cassidy looked up at him and smiled. Her gratitude shone clear on her face. Jovanna's eyes were drooping. Cassidy moved to stand.

Jovanna roused herself. "Mom. Where are you going?"

"Back to the hotel."

"No, stay."

She stroked her daughter's dark hair off her forehead. "All right. I'll stay until you fall asleep."

"No. All night." Jovanna glanced at him and Glendora hovered in the doorway. "In case I have that dream."

Cassidy glanced to Glendora, who nodded her silent consent.

Clyne looked from one woman to the next, miffed that he had not even been consulted.

"All right, doodlebug. I'll stay." She glanced to Clyne and this time she had the smug smile of a poker player holding the winning hand.

CASSIDY STRETCHED OUT on the narrow bed beside her daughter and listened to Amanda tell her about her day from the moment Child Protective Services scooped her up to this moment.

"I'm sorry this is happening to you," said Cassidy.

"It's okay now, Mom. I want to be here. But I want you here, too."

"That's not the way it works. The court has ordered you to stay with them. I'm not allowed to stay here. It's just that your grandmother thought I could help. You understand. It's just for tonight."

Amanda clung tighter. She stroked her daughter's hair and Amanda settled. Her breathing grew steady and her eyelids drooped.

"Don't leave, Mom. Don't sneak out when I fall asleep."

"All right. I'll stay."

"Promise?" asked Amanda.

"Promise."

Amanda drifted to sleep and Cassidy lay in the room that smelled like wool, cedar and old dog. Were these scents familiar to her daughter? When Amanda rolled to her side, Cassidy slipped off the bed and across the room. She needed to find a bathroom.

Buster lifted his head at her departure but did not move from the rug beside her daughter's bed. Cassidy regarded him, trying to decide if he was a threat. Finally she retrieved her gun and holster from the bookcase near the door and slipped the holster on before retreating to the hall. She closed the door softly behind her.

"Is she asleep?"

The male voice made her jump clear off the ground. The corridor was dark and he stood in shadows, leaning against the opposite wall. A shaft of light stabbed across the runner in the hall, supplied by a lamp in the living room.

Clyne, she realized. Now her heart accelerated for a different reason. She pressed a hand over her racing heart and felt the strap of her lace bra beneath her blouse. A tingling ache grew inside her.

He stepped forward, his face all shadows and hard angles.

"Yes."

"Are you staying?"

"I promised that I would."

He nodded and motioned to the door behind him. "I put your things in here. Coat. Briefcase.

It's Gabe's room but he's at the station tonight. And…I gave you one of my T-shirts because my grandmother said you would need it."

"Thank you." Why wasn't she moving?

"Do you need anything else from me?" he asked.

She felt the question was intentionally leading, an offer to finish what they had started in her hotel. She took a little too long answering and his nostrils flared as if catching her scent.

"Nothing," she managed to say, her mouth now dry as dust.

He lifted his chin and she wondered if he was brave enough to take what they both wanted but also knew was just a really rotten idea.

"Thank you for the shirt."

"Bathroom is right down there. My room is there." He pointed and she wondered if this was another invitation.

"I'll be sure not to mix them up."

He lifted his brows. "My grandmother is on the other side of the house, past the living room. So if Amanda has a bad dream, I don't think she would hear the noise."

She didn't take the bait. "I'll be with her."

"Protecting her at night and me all day." He lifted a hand and stroked her cheek. "Chasing away bad dreams."

Her body trembled but she managed to hold

her ground. Unfortunately she didn't step past him or retreat into the spare room. What kind of game was he playing?

"We're talking about Amanda's nightmares. Right?"

He glanced away. Suddenly she didn't think Amanda was the only one who was afraid.

"Gerard had them. I did, too. No shame in it."

"You?" he asked.

"I got some help. No shame in that either. But if you're asking me to tuck you in, I'm going to have to say no."

"I want more than that, Cassidy. I think you do, too."

"What about your reputation?" she asked. "Pillar of the community. Tribal leader. Bastion of Apache culture." She hoped he heard the contempt in her words. She didn't like being treated like an undesirable merely because of her race.

"I will need to choose soon. There are several women who are interested. All Apache women."

"So why point out your bedroom to me?"

He stepped closer. "Because you are different."

She flipped her blond hair. "I'll say."

He took hold of her arm. "No, Cassidy. I don't mean the way you look or the way you smell or your choice of undergarments, which are… memorable. And though you are a beautiful woman. It's deeper than that. You know. You understand what it was like."

And then it made sense, the thing that none of the other women of his tribe could offer. They had not seen action in the Middle East. They had not experienced a war and survived and none of them had lost loved ones to that terrible war.

"How do you do it?" he asked.

"What?"

"Keep fighting?"

"Because it's not over," she said.

"It will never be over," he said. "Just like the battle to keep our land and our heritage. The struggle stretches through generations."

He looked away, staring into the darkness.

"That's true," he said at last.

"Luke says you don't carry a personal weapon. That you don't hunt."

"I have done enough hunting for a lifetime."

"But someone is trying to kill you. You should take some steps to protect yourself."

"No."

"You might die."

"Yes. But I will not die with a gun in my hand."

They shared a moment of silence as each considered their choice. To wear a gun. To set it aside forever.

"Do you remember them all?" she asked.

He met her intent gaze. "Every one. And that's not all. I remember the weather, the location, the moment just before I squeezed that trigger." He sighted an imaginary rifle and looked through his imaginary scope. Then he moved his index finger and made the sound of the discharge. Cassidy flinched. He lowered his hands to his sides.

"You?"

"I remember. The second one was worse. Parker refused to put down his weapon. He pointed it toward me and I fired twice to mass."

He took her hand.

"And I remember the smell of blood and the sound of him trying to breathe with two punctured lungs."

"It's easy to take a life," he said. "Hard to live with, though. You understand that."

This was what attracted him, he realized. What made her different from all the rest of the women in his life. Cassidy knew what it was to fight to defend her life and live with the aftermath.

"But I saw someone afterward. A counselor. It helped, Clyne. You should try it."

His hand slipped from hers. "I don't think so."

"They have a program, some of the counselors are vets. They've seen action. They understand. They don't judge you. Just help you talk it out. I have a connection there."

He hesitated, actually considering it. Then he shook his head.

"I'd go with you if you'd like."

He checked to see if there was some joke associated with her offer, some smirk or facial expression. All he saw was earnestness and compassion. It was his undoing.

Clyne turned away, giving her his back.

She came up beside him, rested a hand on his shoulder. "You did as you were ordered, Clyne. You did what you had to and you came home alive. That has to count."

He turned and lifted her chin with the crook of his index finger.

"Part of me didn't come back," he said and dropped his hand to his side.

She gave him a fragile smile. "Most of you did."

He thought of her husband, the tank commander. He had not been so lucky. He'd lost his life and his family and this beautiful compelling woman standing so close he could feel the heat of her body.

"Clyne, I know you had a terrible assignment. Gerard did, too. He killed people with those tanks. Maybe more than you did."

"He didn't have to look at them."

"Yes. He did. From inside his armored vehicle, he did. I know because he told me. And I saw some of them, too. The wounded. Transported some along with our soldiers."

"Did we make any difference or did we just make more enemies and orphans?"

She had asked herself that very thing. "We made a difference and enemies and orphans. They're still out there, coming for us, Clyne. They still want to do what they did in New York. That's why I still fight. That's why I want to get to out east. I want to stop that from happening again. I want to stop them from killing another American."

Clyne cocked his head. "Are you fighting for a cause, Cassidy, or for revenge?"

She drew back. "Does it matter?"

"Only to me. I had a brother who once sought revenge."

She knew exactly who he meant because she had read his file. Kino Cosen had joined the Shadow Wolves of Immigration and Custom's Enforcement and tracked smugglers but he was there to find his father's killer.

"He got him, too. The very man who took your dad. Must have felt good."

Clyne's mouth tipped down. "He said it didn't feel good. He told me that he didn't kill that man. In the end he forgave him and made his peace."

"The report said…" She thought back, recalling the autopsy report. Snake venom. Why had she thought Kino had killed the Viper?

"Seems I can't forgive myself and you can't forgive the men who took your husband."

That was about it, she realized. "You think sleeping together will clear all that up, do you?"

"No. But it's a connection. That is rare enough." He stroked her cheek. "Takes it beyond the physical. I'm tired of sleeping with women who do not know me inside. They see a leader. I see a killer. You at least recognize me for what I am."

"You were a soldier, Clyne. So was I. It's no shame."

"I thought if I came home and if I did enough for my people that I could again return to the Red Road."

"Red Road?"

"It is the proper way to live and die. Indian people follow this path, the natural way."

"Killing one's enemies should be part of that way." She cupped his jaw in both of her hands. "You might not ever forgive yourself, Clyne. But I forgive you and I thank you for fighting."

The hot tear rolled down his cheek and seeped between her fingers and his jaw.

Then she lifted up on her toes and gave him the kind of kiss she had dreamed of giving her husband when he returned from overseas. A kiss to welcome a soldier home.

Chapter Thirteen

Clyne deepened the kiss as he dragged Cassidy against him. She molded to him as if this was where she was meant to be. Then he realized it was his longing he felt, his need for this woman, too long denied because he knew that she could not be so easily set aside. Because Cassidy knew the warrior's way. She had made an unusual choice and she had continued the fight. Nothing was more important to her except her daughter.

"Do we know what we're doing?" he asked.

She shook her head. "I don't think so."

She stroked his shoulders, her fingers kneading the muscles there, wordlessly seeking contact.

Suddenly he felt like some dreadful cliché. Tarzan with his Jane, King Kong entranced by Fay Wray, the cover of every one of those romance novels that showed a naked warrior gripping a nearly naked blonde and had the word *savage* emblazoned on the cover.

"I don't date white women."

She cocked her head. "This isn't a date."

He still felt the need to qualify. "I'm going to marry an Apache woman. Someone who understands our culture and our ways and can help me lead our people."

She shrugged.

"I didn't want you to think..." His words fell away at the open look of invitation she cast him.

"I don't."

She raked both hands through her fine hair that fell immediately back to place. "I have been without a man for a long time, Clyne. And I haven't missed it. You make me miss the heat and the friction. You make me wonder and fantasize. Maybe it is because we are alike or because we are different. But this attraction is something new. I've never had a battle like this before."

"Is this a battle we need to fight?" he asked.

"Yes, because I'm not sure sleeping with you will make this need go away."

"It might," he said.

"What if it doesn't?"

What, indeed.

The tingle of danger mixed with his arousal increased the ache.

The connection of Jovanna meant they would never be totally rid of each other. Unless his sister chose to stay with Cassidy. That was what Gabe believed would happen. It was why he pushed so hard to have Cassidy here on Black Mountain.

Clyne thought of Jovanna's tears. Gabe had been right.

His brother didn't see the battle. He saw the compromise. Clyne was a master of compromise. Why hadn't he seen it with this woman?

Was it only because he wanted her and so needed her as far away from himself as possible?

Her eyes beckoned, issuing an invitation he could not resist. Her arms circled his waist.

"This will not solve anything," he said.

She agreed with a nod and stepped closer, offering her mouth. "It will make everything worse."

She was right. Whatever it was between them was strong and growing stronger. And he knew the best way to get rid of this kind of unwelcome physical need was to get it over with. The rodeo circuit had taught him that much. Lots of tension. Lots of heat and lots of mornings creeping from a hotel bedroom with his boots in his hands.

She could stop him if she wanted. This

woman looked at him as many women did. But the difference was that he wanted her, too.

His mouth descended. She met him with a kiss filled with passion and need. Her fingers raked over his shoulders as her tongue danced with his. The urgency and the heat surprised him.

He captured her, pressing them together. Cassidy broke the contact of their kiss and turned away. Her eyes closed and he saw the fine blue veins that threaded across her lids.

"We're in a custody battle," she said as if she needed to remind herself as much as him.

"We are."

"Opponents. I'm not doing anything that will hurt my case."

He drew back. "Cassidy, in six months Jovanna will have to choose. Sleeping with me won't change that."

But she was already slipping from his arms. He let her go.

She disappeared into the bathroom. He heard the water run, the toilet flush and the water again. He should go, but he lingered like the love-sick calf that he was.

Clyne did not want to think about why she made him ache all over. Not just in the obvious places, but down deep in his gut and up in his chest. This was about more than sex. That alone should send him running in the opposite direction.

The door opened and she slipped past him again and into Gabe's room. He watched her go and wondered if he was falling for this little white warrior woman. She reappeared with the shirt she had given her, neatly folded and clutched to her chest. Then she eased Jovanna's door open and cast a glance back at him, then into the room. He saw her stiffen and reach. A instant later she held her pistol.

CASSIDY CAUGHT MOVEMENT and reached for the gun as she retreated a step. Her gaze pinned on the possible threat. The dark shape squatted beside her daughter's bed.

And then her brain made sense of the image. Not some person creeping on the floor, she realized, but the dog. He stood and stretched, performing that unique bow used only by dogs. He sauntered to her and used his head to brush her hand. She stooped to thump him on the side.

"Good dog, Buster," Cassidy whispered and holstered her gun.

Behind her, Clyne filled the doorway, blocking out the light and casting a long shadow across the floor.

Buster preceded her to Amanda's bed, then turned in a tight circle on the rug and curled upon the floor. The dog sighed and then lowered his head, allowing Cassidy to approach her daughter's bed.

Amanda slept on her side, facing the wall, her breathing even and deep and the stuffed elephant clutched to her chest. A toy of her childhood. The childhood that Cassidy had no part of.

She sensed rather than heard his approach. She turned to find Clyne halfway across the room, tall and imposing. His presence a comfort.

"Everything all right?"

She nodded, smiling and was rewarded with one of his in return. If possible, it only made him look more appealing.

"I forgot Buster was in here," she whispered. "She never had a dog. Always wanted one."

"She remembered Buster."

Cassidy believed that was so. He drew closer.

"She okay?" he whispered, moving to stand beside her. It reminded her of Gerard, somehow, coming to stand beside their new daughter's miniature bed after they brought her home. In those few precious months between his first and second deployment, they would stand together and watch Amanda sleep.

Cassidy felt her throat constricting at the losses. Clyne's family losing this child and she losing her husband. Was it possible to give Amanda the home she deserved away from the family that loved her? She suddenly did not know what to do and that frightened her.

"Will you promise to keep her safe when I'm gone?"

"You going somewhere?"

She glanced at him but found his expression unreadable. "Well, I can't stay in Amanda's bedroom forever."

He neither argued nor affirmed her comment. Just stared at her with dark, unblinking eyes.

"Don't forget she's just a child," Cassidy whispered. "A child who should not have to make this choice."

Her eyes closed and she held her hands laced together before her mouth as if in prayer.

Cassidy opened her eyes and exited the room, waiting for Clyne to follow. He met her in the hallway and she closed the door.

"When she chooses me, and she will, you will let her go? Drop all your attempts to take her from me?"

His jaw went hard and the muscles of his chest bunched. She held her ground, determined as a badger facing a wolf. His size didn't intimidate her. She'd fight him to the last breath if she must.

"She would lose everything," he said. "Her

connection to a people and a place. Her identity. Her legacy. She is Bear clan. Born of Eagle."

"I don't know what that means."

"Exactly my point. You don't. Jovanna must relearn the language of her people. Begin her training so she will be ready for her Sunrise Ceremony."

Cassidy's eyes narrowed. "The womanhood thing? She's a girl. She just bought her first tub of pink lip gloss, for goodness' sakes."

"So it's already begun, her transition to a woman."

"Hardly." But the signs were there. The interest in boys and her abandonment of the childish toys that once were so important.

"I spoke about Changing Woman. Jovanna will become her during the ceremony. Not pretend to be her, she will be her. And she will dance and pray. We will all pray for her to become the best possible woman."

"Are there drugs involved? Peyote or some such, because I will bust you, all of you, so fast."

Clyne rolled his eyes. "You see. This is the trouble. You don't know anything about us."

"I know it's illegal to give drugs to a minor."

"We won't."

"Fine. Dress her up in feathers and beads. It won't change her." She scowled at him. "I just want my daughter back so I can get her out of here."

Now Clyne scowled. "What is so wrong with Black Mountain?"

"Let's see." She lifted her hand to tick off the reasons on each finger. "Unemployment rate. Dropout rate. Teen pregnancy rate. Violence against women." She ran out of fingers. "Oh, yeah, and a major drug syndicate."

Clyne's expression fell. "But she belongs in this place. You can't take her away from here."

"Not yet I can't. But once this ridiculous separation is over and she makes her choice, I surely can and you can't stop us."

"Why? Why is it so important to take her away from the place of her ancestors?"

"Because I need to get to a real field office. One where I can do some good instead of busting bank robbers, kidnappers and drug traffickers."

"Real? What does that even mean?"

"Where the bad guys are. The important ones."

"You mean Al-Qaeda, ISIS?"

"Yes."

"In other words, terrorists."

One brow lifted and he considered her for a long moment. "You know that the illegal immigrants have included members of both of those organizations, right here in Arizona."

"And the cases are made in NY and DC. I need to be a part of that."

"Why?"

She didn't answer. She'd already told him too much. Cassidy turned to leave him but he took hold of her elbow, urging her to face him.

"Why, Cassidy. Why ISIS and Al-Qaeda?"

She threw the words at him, hurling them from deep down inside herself where she had kept them alive, burning like a coal ember.

"Because those are the men who killed Gerard."

She slapped her hand over her mouth as her eyes rounded. She had not meant to tell him that.

He reached for her and she shuffled back, letting her hand slip from her mouth.

"Good night, Clyne."

He stopped his advance. "Cassidy, wait."

She didn't, instead she made a quick march back to her daughter's room. Sometimes retreat was the best course of action.

Cassidy closed the door and lay her pistol and shoulder holster on the book shelf. Then she quickly undressed, leaving on only her panties and then slipping into the overlong T-shirt. The cotton was soft and clean and smelled of soap. It wasn't until she was standing beside the closed wooden door that she looked down at the T-shirt he had provided for her. It read: I ♥ Rez Boys.

Cassidy let out a groan. She forced herself to march across the room and slipped in beside her slumbering daughter. She forced herself to stillness as she recalled Clyne's earthy scent and his words. Why was it so important to take her away from her home, her people and her tribe? To say she slept would be a mistake. Dozed, roused, listened, dozed, from well after midnight until the early hours before morning.

She woke to a noise similar to the high-pitched whine that alerted her to one of Amanda's nightmares. She was already halfway out of bed when she realized she slept beside her daughter. The whine became a shout. But it was not Amanda. That was the voice of a man and he was screaming.

Cassidy's ears pinned back at the ferociousness and she crept across the floor to retrieve her pistol, removed the safety and headed for the door.

Chapter Fourteen

Cassidy slipped into the hallway. Someone was already there. The light flicked on and Cassidy recognized Glendora, her expression startled as she took in the picture of Cassidy in the hallway gripping her pistol.

"What is that sound?" asked Cassidy. Then she realized that the shouts came from Clyne's room.

"He has nightmares ever since coming home," said Glendora, motioning to Clyne's room.

Cassidy slid the safety back in place and lowered her weapon. Glendora shuffled past her and knocked on the door.

"Mama?"

Cassidy recognized her daughter's voice coming from her new room. She went to her daughter, finding her sitting up wide-eyed in bed. Buster was no longer on the floor, but sitting beside her daughter on the mattress as Amanda clung to his shaggy coat.

"It's all right, doodlebug. Your brother Clyne is having a nightmare."

It was the first time she'd called him Amanda's brother and the realization brought her up short.

"He has nightmares, too?" Amanda's grip on Buster loosened.

Cassidy sat on the bed.

"Are they about breaking glass?" Amanda's therapist thought the breaking glass dream stemmed from some early childhood experience. Now Cassidy understood, it was the car crash. Amanda had been in the accident that had killed Tessa Cosen.

"I don't know. Maybe you can ask him tomorrow."

The shouts stopped and the house went quiet. A few moments later she heard Clyne's door shut and Amanda's open.

"You two all right?" asked Glendora.

"We're fine, Gramma," piped Amanda.

Glendora offered another good-night and left them.

Cassidy stretched out beside her daughter. "What do you think of them?" she asked Amanda.

"I love them," she said instantly. They were

quiet for a time and she thought Amanda had dozed off when she spoke again. "Mama?"

"Yes."

"Would it… Could you… Will you call me Jovanna from now on?"

Cassidy felt the stabbing pain as some deep part of herself began screaming.

"Why do you want that, doodlebug?"

"Well. It's my name. The name my first mother gave me."

"Oh, I see." She held back the burning in her throat and thought her words sounded almost normal. "Well, I can try. But you might have to remind me sometimes."

"Okay. Thank you, Mama." Her arms came around Cassidy's neck.

Cassidy held her daughter, wishing that Amanda could have her brothers and her grandmother and still stay with her forever. She thought of Clyne and his insistence that he marry an Apache woman. Of Gerard promising to come home. Things didn't always go as you hoped. Amanda's arms slipped from her neck as her daughter cuddled in her bedding, settling for sleep.

Cassidy might be different from other women in his life and she understood some of the issues he faced as a vet. They might even share a physical connection that she knew was unique.

But there was one thing they did not share—his heritage. And no matter what she did, there was just no way she could ever become Apache.

CASSIDY WOKE AND checked her watch. It was a little past six. She eased from her daughter's bed and headed for the hallway, pausing only to retrieve her pistol from the bookshelf. Then she continued to the bathroom at the end of the hall. She opened the door and paused at the billowing steam and the scent of soap and shaving cream. Clyne stood naked before the bathroom mirror with a white towel slung over his neck and his bronze skin made even darker in contrast to the white shaving cream covering one side of his face. He held a razor in one hand and the other gripped the sink.

Cassidy squeezed the doorknob as her entire body leaped from drowsiness to tingling awareness. Clyne Cosen naked was a better stimulant than a double shot of espresso.

"I'm sorry," she muttered.

Clyne startled and then whipped the towel off his shoulders and threw it around his hips.

"I didn't know. It wasn't locked." She forced her gaze to his face.

He gripped the towel with one hand and pressed the other to his chest.

"Didn't hear you." He blew out a breath. "Thought it was Jovanna for a minute."

She tore her gaze away and looked at the door, seeing there was no latch.

"No lock?" she asked.

"Shut is occupied in this house. I'm sorry no one told you." Cassidy retreated so fast she stumbled into the hall. Clyne tucked in the edge of the towel, fixing it in place. He was naked except for a narrow band of terry cloth. She thought he looked even more appealing with his muscular frame damp from the shower and his wet hair clinging to his wide shoulders. He showered with that small beaded leather pouch, she realized. She had seen the sodden leather nestled just below the hollow of his throat. Something else she didn't understand, she realized.

"Do you carry that thing everywhere?" he asked, pointing his razor at her pistol.

"Nearly."

"I'll be out in a second." He let his gaze sweep down her exposed legs and then returned his attention to her face. The look he gave her could have steamed the mirror.

"We're in trouble. Aren't we?" she asked.

Clyne didn't look at her. "Cassidy, am I the guy you want to introduce to your family?"

His tone was sarcastic. Her answer was not.

"I don't have any family except Amanda."

When he looked at her again, the heat was gone, replaced by a look of pity.

"No one?" he asked.

She swallowed but the lump continued to rise in her throat, so she shook her head in answer. Then she closed the door, removing the sight of his jaw dropping open. Of course he couldn't imagine that, no clan or tribe or community. No huge loving family. No place that was home.

She didn't care. Home wasn't a place anyway.

Cassidy returned to her room and dressed, waiting until she heard Clyne leave the bathroom and the sound of his bedroom door clicking shut before she ventured out into the hall and into the bathroom.

It still smelled like soap and aftershave.

When she reached the kitchen a few minutes later it was to find Clyne dressed in polished, elaborately stitched cowboy boots, dark jeans and a deep blue button-up shirt cinched at the throat with a chunk of turquoise the size of a quail's egg. The long wet hair was now contained in a neat braid secured with a bit of red cloth. His gray blazer sat on the back of the chair.

He glanced up at her and motioned to the seat across from his. His presence so captivated her that she hardly noticed his grandmother, dressed in black knit pants, white blouse and pale blue cardigan sweater.

"How you like your coffee?" asked Glendora, sliding a mug before her.

"Black," said Cassidy. "Thank you."

Glendora nodded. "Same as Gabe and Kino. I think all police drink coffee black. No fuss. Right?" She motioned to her eldest grandson. "This one drinks it with milk. Lots of milk. Good thing I still have some cows!" She turned back to the stove. "I'm making potatoes, scrambled eggs and bacon. But then I remembered that Jovanna doesn't eat meat. So I don't know what to do. I never cooked for a vegetarian before. I generally use the bacon grease for the potatoes and eggs."

Cassidy stood, tentatively approaching the stove. "I can make her breakfast. She likes fried eggs and toast."

They spent a few minutes discussing her daughter's diet until Glendora felt more comfortable.

"Last night, she asked me to call her Jovanna," Cassidy announced.

Clyne and Glendora stared.

Glendora clasped her hands together. "She did!"

"She said that was what her first mom named her."

"First mom?" Clyne said, his brow lifting as

he replaced his coffee to the table. "That's what she called her?"

Glendora bustled as she spoke. "The lady from Child Welfare will be here soon. She's taking Jovanna to school and she said she'd be back after school to check in, too."

Buster appeared and stood by the back door. Clyne let him out by opening the door without moving from his place. A moment later Amanda emerged in the doorway. *Jovanna*, Cassidy corrected herself.

She had already dressed in the same clothing she wore yesterday. She accepted greetings from them all and sat between Clyne and Cassidy. Buster scratched at the door and spent breakfast eating the crusts of toast offered by Jovanna.

Her daughter munched her toast and sipped her milk. Then she eyed Clyne and said.

"Are your nightmares about breaking glass?"

Clyne choked on his coffee, narrowly missing spilling on his pristine shirt.

"Did I wake you?" he asked.

"Yes. I was scared, but Mommy came right in. I have them, too. I hear glass breaking and screaming and I wake up."

Clyne looked to Glendora. Had they both correctly guessed at the root of this particular dream? Clyne turned his attention back to his sister.

"Mine are about the time I was a soldier."

"My father was a soldier, too. He was killed in action by an IED. That's an…"

"Improvised explosive device," said Clyne.

"That's right!" said Jovanna.

Clyne's complexion had taken on a green tinge. He knew IEDs. That much was certain. Had he seen one detonate or stopped someone who carried one?

"I wish he was still alive. You two could be friends."

Clyne and Cassidy exchanged a look. It was doubtful that Amanda's father and Amanda's brother would have ever been friends.

"Right, Mama?"

"I think they have a lot in common."

Amanda munched her toast, slipping another crust under the table, where it vanished. The sound of Buster chewing came an instant later.

Child Welfare arrived on time and Cassidy kissed her daughter goodbye. She called Diane to check in and asked her to overnight a box of clothing to Clyne's address and Diana said she had sent a box yesterday to her hotel address. They should arrive today. That was a relief because her daughter was not wearing the same thing to the reservation school tomorrow.

Buster scratched at the door, and Clyne let him out and then called to Glendora.

"I think Buster is following Jovanna to school."

Cassidy looked out the back door and saw Buster tearing down the drive and out onto the road.

"I'll go after him," he said and turned to Cassidy. "Want to see the school?"

She did. They left together in her car. On the way she asked if he would be willing to translate some of Manny Escalanti's phone conversations and he agreed. They finished the lot before reaching the school.

"What do you think?" she asked, regarding her careful notes.

"Well, the brown rabbit might be his way of speaking about Ronnie Hare. He said he'd gone for a run and that he was a bad swimmer."

"Swimmer?"

"Might mean he's not willing to cross back over the Salt River to our reservation or that he's not willing to leave the reservation to go to Mexico."

"He said his cousins are taking care of the rabbit," said Cassidy. "Is that bringing him supplies or is that an order to kill him?"

Clyne gave her a long look. "I don't know. But if it were me, I'd want Ronnie Hare dead.

He was the messenger between Escalanti and the Mexican drug lords."

"Who is bringing messages now? I wonder."

"Good question. Either way, you guys better bring him in quick." Clyne pulled into the school lot. There sat Buster, before one of the string of windows on the side of the building. "There he is."

"Is that her classroom?"

"If Buster says so. That dog lost her once. He's not letting her go a second time."

Cassidy thought that Clyne and Buster had a lot in common.

Clyne called Buster but he had to carry the dog to the car.

Cassidy stood beside her vehicle staring at the window Buster had chosen. How many times had Amanda had to begin again? Be the new kid who started months after everyone else with a new teacher and a new set of requirements? Six? Seven? How many more times was she going to pick up her daughter and move her like, what had Clyne said, as if she was a canary?

Six months. It wouldn't be enough to set down roots. Not the kind that sank deep, those that took a lifetime to grow. And her daughter had only—

"Six months," she whispered.

Clyne stood beside her, holding the giant dog

as if he were a puppy instead of a senior citizen with a white muzzle.

"Cassidy, it's fair. Six months with us after nine years with you. Give your daughter a chance to know us."

"It's too much. A child shouldn't have to choose between two families." She should never have to choose. She should be able to have her mother and her family. But how?

"The courts make them do it every day. You know it. I know it."

Cassidy looked at him with big blue eyes, brimming with tears. It hurt to look at her, but he couldn't look away. Clyne knew the face of grief, intimately.

"What if she chooses you?" she whispered.

And there it was, the reason she had fought so hard to keep her child.

"She's all I have, Clyne. You have brothers, their wives, your grandmother. Your whole tribe." She looked away. "She's all I have in the world."

"Gabe says you are a part of Jovanna, because you raised her. That's why he wanted you here."

"And maybe for me to see the family I am keeping her from," said Cassidy.

Clyne gave her a lot of credit for admitting that.

He opened the door and let Buster into the

backseat. Then he opened her door and waited for her to take her seat. She handed over the keys.

She didn't recall him starting the sedan, but the speed bump leaving the school grounds snapped her back to the present. She looked at him and he glanced to her and back to the road. Behind them Buster panted and paced across the backseat.

"Is it a good school?"

"I went there. My brothers, too. Lots of our kids go on to college. Jovanna can take advanced classes at the high school later on."

"She won't be here that long."

He said nothing to that.

"Tell me about the Sunrise Ceremony," she said.

Clyne looked out at the road as he tried to think back to the last ceremony he attended instead of the woman beside him. Cassidy had moved past a distraction. She hadn't even mentioned their exchange last night. But he couldn't stop thinking about her, them. He was in trouble. Big trouble.

"Clyne?"

"Yes. I'm thinking." About the fuchsia underthings worn by this field agent and former army evac pilot.

He described the ceremony that took place

each July Fourth. He did not tell her that it was the same day that his mother had died and his sister had been lost.

Instead he described the chanting prayer and the drumming of the males of the family and all of the families coming from other reservations. The gifts given and received. The feasting and music and dance. The sacred objects and the bee pollen to be sprinkled on Jovanna by the medicine man to bring prosperity, fertility and health. But there were gaps. Parts of the ceremony were secret to outsiders and others secret from the Apache men. Even he did not know what Jovanna's mentor would teach her during their time of seclusion, only that it involved the mysteries of womanhood.

"She will dance through an entire night and greet the rising sun, still dancing."

Cassidy frowned. "Isn't that too much to ask of a little girl?"

"No. It's a test of strength and she won't be alone. Others will dance with her. Her mentor, grandmother and sisters. Then she'll sleep a little and there will be feasting. Finally the Crown Dancers will dance when she becomes Changing Woman."

Her voice turned wistful. "I'd like to see Amanda dance."

He didn't correct her or call his sister by her

given name, but he thought that Cassidy should be there. That Gabe was right to want to include this woman in Jovanna's inner circle. Did it make them less her family to have Cassidy as her mother?

He wondered what his own mother would advise him? He knew that she would want what was best for Jovanna. But what was that?

Chapter Fifteen

Luke called that afternoon to announce a major break. Cassidy was reviewing the transcripts from Manny Escalanti with Chief Cosen when Luke reported that he had caught Ronald Hare at the food drop he'd been scouting in Salt River. They now had in custody a man who could testify against several of the big players on both reservations and confirm exactly which cartel they were dealing with. That was *if* he was willing to play ball. If not, he was going to prison.

Cassidy knew that it would be up to the Salt River tribal council whether to try Hare in tribal court or turn him over to federal jurisdiction. Now the transcripts she was accumulating on Manny Escalanti took on new urgency. Luke had made certain that Hare's arrest was public because he wanted to see the rats scatter.

Late in the afternoon, she collected a large

box from the hotel. Amanda's clothes. She breathed a sigh of relief.

Now she had an excuse to stop by the Cosens' again. She glanced at her watch. Amanda would be home from school by now. Cassidy was dying to hear about her first day.

Perhaps she could stay the night again. A perfect image of Clyne naked except for that white towel burst across her mind like the finale of a fireworks display. He was that breathtaking.

Eventually she would have to move back to the hotel.

Six months without Amanda. How would she do it? Of course she had to eventually move back to Phoenix and she wasn't about to move to DC or New York with Amanda being a captive of the Apache tribe.

Bear born of Eagle, he had said. What did that even mean? Clans, she supposed.

Clyne stopped by to speak with Gabe but as he entered his brother's office, his gaze moved immediately to her. She stood as he paused, noticing every last detail about him. His hair was in one braid today, wrapped in maroon cloth overlaid with a crisscrossing series of leather cords. She could barely manage a clip in her hair and he'd managed that.

He lifted his gaze and it locked with hers. Her stomach twitched and her skin turned to gooseflesh in excitement. Who was she kidding? She wasn't stopping this man from walking across the hall and over her threshold. Not for long. It was just a matter of time. He knew it and she knew it.

This was bad.

She dragged her gaze away and met Gabe's speculative eyes. His gaze flicked to Clyne and then back to her. She could see the suspicion solidifying to certainty. He lifted his brows and her ears went hot.

Clyne finally noticed his brother's scrutiny. The corners of his mouth drooped.

"What?" Clyne said.

"Nothing," said Gabe. Then he lifted his finger and aimed it at his older brother. "But I don't want to hear one more word about Selena's father and how marrying her will ruin my reputation."

"I don't know what you're talking about," said Clyne.

But his color rose with the denial.

"No? Maybe I don't need to sleep on my office couch tonight. Maybe my bedroom is free."

Cassidy looked to Clyne to see how he wanted to play this.

"It's not free," he said.

"But it might be?"

Clyne didn't deny it.

"Oh, great!" said Gabe. "Just great." He pointed at Cassidy and kept his eyes locked with Clyne's. "This is the kind of thing I'd expect from Kino or Clay. But you? I don't believe it. She's a federal agent. She's white. She's fighting us for custody."

Clyne rounded on his brother. "You're the one who said to bring her here. Include her in our family."

"I didn't mean you should sleep with her!"

"I haven't," he said.

"Yet," said Gabe.

Heads in the squad room snapped up. She wished she could sink through the floor, and Clyne seemed to have turned to stone. His eyes shifted to Gabe and just his hand moved as he closed the door to his office.

"What do you think you're doing?" Clyne asked.

"What, you think it will stay a secret? Your assistant already told Yepa that you took her to lunch."

Cassidy had met Yepa, Gabe's personal assistant.

"You were seen with her at the casino hotel, leaving her room. Plus Yepa's brother drives the school bus and saw her car in the drive a little too early this morning."

"Jovanna didn't take the bus," said Cassidy.

Gabe shook his head as she missed the point. Black Mountain was a small community and they had already made the list of interesting doings here.

What was that buzzing sound?

Cassidy's phone vibrated across Gabe's desk. Conversation stopped. The phone buzzed again. She lunged and scooped up the device.

Phone in hand, Cassidy checked the ID and saw it was her boss.

"Agent Walker, here."

Tully skipped the pleasantries and got right to business.

"We pulled a partial from the rifle casing on the roof in Tucson and got a match."

Cassidy stuck a finger in her opposite ear to better hear the results. This caused both brothers to shift their attention to her. Clyne and Gabe moved in.

"Who?" she asked.

"Johnny Parker."

"Parker?" She raked her nails through the hair at her temple as the pieces still did not fit. "Should I know that name?"

"He's the brother of Brett Parker. Your case. Kidnapping."

Brett Parker. *That* name she knew immediately. Johnny was the kidnapper's brother. She turned to Clyne to see his brow furrowed.

"Why would Johnny Parker want to kill Clyne Cosen?"

"He wouldn't. Cassidy, we don't think Cosen is the target. He's after you."

Cassidy clutched the phone as she reeled from this new information.

"Me?" she asked.

Clyne moved beside her. Gabe returned to his desk, his attention fixed on her. Cassidy pressed the phone to her ear.

"Not Cosen?" She shook her head at Clyne.

"We think Johnny Parker picked you up at the Tucson rally. He might have guessed that there would be a strong FBI presence and got lucky. After all, you were right up there on stage."

"How would he know me?"

"We aren't sure. He could have been in court any of the times you testified. Our guys are looking at court surveillance video now."

"The truck. In the garage in Phoenix. Forrest said—"

"I know. He told me. But someone picked up that truck in Black Mountain. He knows you are up there. We need you to get to the safe house. Hare is in custody and Forrest is en route to you. He will meet you there. We're sending our people to you."

"All right." A burst of terror bolted through her. "Wait! My daughter!"

Her eyes locked to Gabe. He picked up his desk phone and started pushing buttons.

"He couldn't have her location," said Tully. "It's not possible."

Cassidy pressed a hand to her forehead. "It *is* possible. I didn't go to the hospital after the shooting. I went home to my daughter."

"What?" Her boss's voice was a roar.

Gabe dropped the handset back to the cradle and headed out the door, scooping up his gray Stetson as he passed the coat rack. Cassidy followed him out with Clyne on her heels.

"And last night. I was at the Cosens'. He could have followed me. He could know where she is."

"Hold on."

She didn't listen and instead broke into a run. She could hear Tully shouting orders to his staff. Then he came back on.

"We're bringing her in."

"She's not at home."

"Where is she?"

"Here on Black Mountain Reservation. Cosen residence. They won temporary custody." She followed Gabe out the squad room, passing him as she ran down the hall. Clyne reached the door first and shouted that his car was closer.

Donald Tully spoke again. "I'll call their police chief."

"He's already on his way to her. I'm en route," she said.

"Cassidy. No. Get to the safe house, now."

"En route," she said.

"You're the target! You might draw him right to her."

Cassidy froze, phone pressed to her ear and stared at Clyne, who with his longer legs had beat her to the car and stood with the door open.

"Go to the safe house," ordered Tully. "We're coming to you."

"No! My daughter. I have someone for protection."

"Who?"

She looked at Clyne, who nodded his consent.

"A US marine sharpshooter."

"Are you talking about Clyne Cosen? He's not protection. He's a civilian. Cassidy, I need you—"

She hung up.

"Get in," said Clyne.

Cassidy shook her head. "You have to get to her. Amanda. Jovanna, I mean. There is someone after me, but they could have followed me to her."

He closed the door. "What about you?"

"I'll go right back into the station."

Clyne swept the parking lot and street with his gaze and then pinned it back on her.

"All right."

Cassidy did something she had never done. Something she knew was against every rule in the book. She removed her personal weapon and offered it to Clyne butt-first. He looked at it as if she had offered him a live rattlesnake. He gave a rapid head shake as he backed away. Then he turned and retreated to his SUV. She watched him pull away and then slipped her weapon back into its holster. She withdrew her cell phone and dialed her daughter.

"Hi, Mom." Her daughter's voice rang like a musical instrument. "What's up?"

"Where are you?"

"At Grandma's house." Her voice was more hesitant now as she picked up the note of panic in her mother's voice.

"Inside?"

"Yes. Mom, what's going on? Is it the Child Protection people again?"

"Put Grandma on."

There was a pause and she heard Jovanna speaking. Then Glendora came on.

"Hello?"

"Glendora. It's Cassidy. Gabe and Clyne are on their way. There is a current active threat against Jovanna. Get to a back bedroom and lock the door. Get on the floor, away from windows. Do you understand?"

"Yes."

"Go."

She heard Glendora speaking to Jovanna. And, bless her heart, her voice was calm and even as she gave instructions. A few moments later Glendora spoke.

"We're locked in. Gabe is calling on my phone," said Glendora. "Here."

There was a brief pause and Jovanna came on again.

"Mom, what's happening?"

"Just wait there. Your brothers are on their way to you. They'll explain."

"I hear sirens," said Jovanna.

Cassidy closed her eyes and breathed a sigh of relief and when she opened her eyes she realized she was standing in the open on the sidewalk before the parking area. Her gaze flicked about, taking in the numerous places where a shooter could hide. Her hand went to her vest and she recalled she had left it in her hotel room last night in her rush to get to her daughter.

Cassidy now stood, unprotected and vulnerable to a shooter. She lowered the phone and ran toward tribal police headquarters.

Chapter Sixteen

There was no one in the yard and the eerie emptiness of the house gave Clyne a chill. He and Gabe pulled in right behind Kino and Clay. Gabe reached the steps and flew into the house, gun raised, shouting for their grandmother. He cleared the entrance as he heard the reply.

"We're here. In my bedroom."

Gabe had reached their grandmother's door and held his gun pointed at the ceiling.

"You both all right?"

Clyne stood shoulder to shoulder with Gabe as Glendora replied. From beneath the door came a familiar huffing sound that Clyne recognized as Buster sniffing them from beneath the door.

"Yes. We're all fine."

"Jovanna?" called Clyne.

"I'm here, too!" she piped, her voice sweet music to his ears. "And Buster."

"You want me to unlock the door?" asked Glendora.

"No," said Gabe. "Stay on the floor. I have to check the area."

He was on his radio now. Kino and Clay remained outside and Gabe ordered them to scout the exterior for any sign of intruders. Clyne knew that there were no better men for the job. Kino and Clay had been excellent trackers before they went down on the border as Shadow Wolves. Now they were the best on the reservation.

Gabe looked to Clyne. "Will you take my shotgun?" he asked.

Clyne felt that cold sweat at just the thought of holding a weapon.

"Never mind. Just stay here until I get back." Gabe darted down the hall.

He watched his brother go and thought of what might have happened. The horrors of the past mingled with the potential threat against his sister. They'd only just got her back. He couldn't lose her again. Yet he wasn't strong enough to pick up a gun to defend her. His mind gave all the rational reasons to go down the hall to Gabe's gun closet, the one in his bedroom. He even made it to the locked cabinet.

But he couldn't open that lock. Oh, he knew where Gabe kept a second key. That wasn't the trouble. The trouble was one particular gun. He thought he might be able to hold a shotgun. But he knew what else was in there because he'd placed it in Gabe's care when he came home. His long-range rifle, the one with thirty-six confirmed kills. Three dozen lives. Most of the ghosts stayed away. But some haunted him. Especially the boy who died with a claymore in his hand, the detonation coming just after Clyne squeezed the trigger and before the youngster could throw the bomb at the US forces. Clyne knew he had to take the shot. But the age of the boy made it wrong in his heart.

Maybe Cassidy was right. He needed to talk to someone.

"Clyne?" called Glendora.

He retreated to his grandmother, his palms slick with sweat. "Cassidy wants a report."

His mouth twitched. "Tell her we are checking the perimeter."

"Okay."

In a few minutes Clay appeared. "Nothing. No tracks and no sign of an intruder. Gabe wants Kino and me to get Jovanna to the safe house."

"Cassidy?" asked Clyne.

"Gabe wants you to bring her." Clay knocked

on the door and then spoke in Apache. "Grandma. Open the door."

The lock clicked and Glendora peered out at them. She ushered her granddaughter out. Buster pushed past him, hugging Jovanna's leg as she moved into the hall. Clay took charge of his sister, guiding her down the hall with Clyne covering their back.

Gabe waited on the front step and Kino held open the door to his police car. Clay scooped Jovanna up as if she were still that two-year-old girl they had lost and ran her to Kino's police cruiser, ducking into the backseat with her. Buster jumped inside before Clyne had the door shut.

"Grandma, you're in the front with Kino," said Gabe to Glendora.

"Let me get my coat."

Gabe waited and then guided his grandmother across the muddy yard to his brother's unit. He saw Glendora seated in the front.

"Luke is en route from Salt River," said Kino to Gabe.

"Good. Take off," ordered Gabe and closed the door.

Clyne watched Kino pull out, lights flashing but without his siren.

Gabe looked to Clyne. "Cassidy?"

Clyne nodded. "I got her." Gabe swept behind

the wheel and Clyne climbed into his SUV. A moment later they were off.

CASSIDY WALKED WITH Clyne up the steps of the safe house. She knew the drab exterior was an illusion. This place had a safe room, supplies and enough communication equipment to make the Apple Store jealous.

It also had weapons. Lots and lots of them.

She entered the code and waited for the door to click. Her daughter called to her and leaped off her seat in the dining room. But Gabe got a hold of her arm, keeping her from charging into the open until Cassidy got Clyne inside and the door shut and bolted.

Buster greeted them first, and then Gabe let Jovanna go. Cassidy met her daughter halfway across the room with a hug so tight she didn't think anything or anyone could break it. Gradually she eased away.

"Are you all right?" she asked.

Jovanna nodded and motioned to her brothers. "They all protected me."

Cassidy tried for a smile as she looked from Glendora to Gabe, to Kino, to Clay and finally to Clyne. But her lip trembled, and she and her words quavered.

"Well, that's what families do," she managed.

Buster nudged between them and used his head to encourage Jovanna to pet him.

"Oh, and Buster, too. Of course," said Jovanna and laughed.

Jovanna and Buster lead her through the dining room. "They have a machine here that makes hot cocoa! Do you want one?"

"Maybe just coffee."

The group moved to the kitchen, where a large couch flanked the counter set with four stools. Kino and Clay took the stools, and Glendora and Clyne sank into the couch. Gabe remained on guard by the metal door that led to the garage, where two vehicles waited, gassed and ready to go.

With Buster beside her like a guard dog, Jovanna showed her mom to the marvelous machine that dispensed coffee and hot cocoa. "Were you scared?" asked Cassidy.

"Only a little. When we were on the floor. But Grandma told me stories about Changing Woman. Did you know she had two sons?" She held up two fingers and ticked them off. "Child of Water and Monster Slayer." She glanced to Glendora, who nodded at this correct reciting. "He's also Killer of Enemies and he made the world safe for us. I wonder what monsters he killed."

The only monster Cassidy cared about right now was Johnny Parker.

"Then Changing Woman got lonely and made the Apache people out of her own flesh." Jovanna gave a little wiggle as if this thought was repellant and Cassidy smiled, thinking that all children are made of their mother's flesh.

"During the Sunrise Ceremony, I'll be Changing Woman and my dance will be a blessing. But first I have to learn a lot of things and start my real education."

Cassidy lifted a brow at Glendora. Jovanna's grandmother certainly had been a busy bee.

The coffeemaker whirred and spit black liquid. Cassidy passed the first cup to Gabe with her thanks and then took orders from the rest of the Cosens. When she finished, she sat at the counter with her daughter, facing Kino and Clay.

"Grandma showed me the buckskin dress," said Jovanna. "It's the most beautiful thing I've ever seen!"

Cassidy smiled at the excitement in her daughter's animated gestures as she described the wonderful garment.

"I'm jealous," said Clay. "Boys don't get to wear something like that. But we'll all dance at your ceremony."

"You will?" She looked from one brother to the next. "All of you?"

"All," said Clyne.

"We'll be dressed as the Ga'an," said Kino, "the four spirits of the mountain."

"But there are five dancers," said Jovanna. "I read about it and watched it online. The crowns are huge! One will wear a white hood. Who will be the fifth?"

They all turned to Clyne for the answer.

"I was going to ask your uncle Luke."

Jovanna smiled and clapped her hands. "Yes!"

Buster settled beneath Jovanna's stool with a slight groan before resting his head on his white-tipped paws. She wondered vaguely what kind of sheepdog he was and decided it didn't matter. He was a good one.

"And your brothers will also beat the drum while you sing."

"Only one drum?" asked Jovanna.

"Only one. But it's a big one," said Glendora. "My grandsons are really good drummers and they have wonderful voices. You'll hear them all singing just for you."

And Kino and Clay's wives and Gabe's girl will all dance with you through the night. Keep you company and encourage you when you get tired."

"My mentors?"

Now how did her daughter know about

that, wondered Cassidy and her gaze flicked to Glendora.

"You will have only one mentor."

"Who?" asked Jovanna.

"Well, she can't be a relative and she must be strong and wise and an Apache, of course," said Glendora.

Cassidy realized all her grandsons were looking to her.

"I would like to ask Selena Dosela."

Clyne's jaw dropped and then snapped shut. Gabe grinned and stood a little taller. A controversial choice, thought Cassidy, recognizing that Clyne was less than pleased. Selena was Gabe's fiancé, but she had also been the driver of the chemicals needed to supply the meth lab in January. Working with Department of Justice, but only because the cartels had threatened her family. Cassidy considered what she would be willing to do to protect Jovanna.

"I like Selena," said Cassidy. "She's nice."

Clyne thought he might need to discuss this choice with his grandmother, but not here or now.

"Three of my boys have found good women."

He met his grandmother's gaze. He knew the look. He had no woman to bring to the ceremony.

Thirty-two was hardly over-the-hill. He had

time still. Time to rise to council chairman and time to choose a wife who would help him lead the tribe with honor and dignity. Rita was a good choice, or Paulina. They were both professional women, accomplished, modest. Karen was the most knowledgeable about their cultural history. They were all suitable and all had made their interest known. So why hadn't he chosen?

His attention strayed to Cassidy. Their gazes locked and he felt the tingle of awareness that made him itch to bring her into his arms. He broke the contact and stared at his coffee and then to his brothers. Clay was watching him with a curious expression.

Glendora was speaking about Clay's wife, Izzie.

"I knew she was the girl for him. Why it took him so long to realize it, I'll never know." She pushed Clyne and he had a time keeping the coffee from sloshing out of the mug onto the arm of the couch. "This one has yet to choose because he's working all the time."

Jovanna giggled at her older brother.

"The oldest. He should set an example and marry a nice Apache girl."

"I will, Grandma," he said, but his gaze fixed on Cassidy. Her expression was a frozen mask, her smile tight as the grip on her coffee.

"You work too hard. That's why you don't

have a girl. You need to dance more and sing more and play the drum like you used to."

It couldn't be Cassidy. He would not allow it to be her.

"I still play the drum and sing."

"At ceremonies. What about your flute? You used to play all the time."

What had happened to his flute? He didn't even know. In a box somewhere with the things his mother had packed when she moved his belongings from their father's house while he'd been deployed in Iraq. Despite the hot coffee in his hand, Clyne felt cold.

His grandmother noticed something immediately. Her face now held the etched lines of concern. "What's wrong?"

"Nothing."

Glendora gave him a long look and then she began talking to Jovanna about the beading of the moccasins she would make and how her sisters would come up from Salt River to help with the cooking.

"There will be hundreds of guests. On Thursday we will all dance and sing, and I'll feed everyone with the help of my sisters and Kino, Clay and Gabe's girls. The men will prepare the sacred objects. You will meet with the medicine man and your mentor for instruction. Friday you will have to run around the gifts that people bring you and you'll give them gifts, too. Then you and Selena will prepare for your longest dance. All Friday night and, if you are strong, you will still be dancing when the sun rises."

"All night?" asked Jovanna, a note of concern in her voice.

"Um-hm. And then you will rest and later Selena will massage your back and legs, molding you into a new woman."

Jovanna's eyes were wide. Cassidy listened with a mixture of awe and worry.

"There will be a blessing and then you will dance in the dress I showed you."

"Changing Woman," said Jovanna and smiled.

"People will come from everywhere to see you dance and receive your blessing."

Clyne watched Cassidy as she stroked her daughter's hair and sipped her coffee. As she began to relax, so did he. She glanced at him and cast him a smile. He sent it back and saw her cheeks flush. That made his smile broaden. Was she thinking of last night and the kisses they had shared? He lifted his mug, but kept his eyes on her as the memories warmed him.

Gradually he noticed that his grandmother had ceased talking. His eyes rounded and he turned to glance at her to find her gaping at him.

Now he flushed.

"What?" he asked.

Glendora's gaze flipped to Cassidy and then back to him. She lifted a brow in silent inquiry and looked to Gabe, who nodded. His grandmother frowned. So much for keeping their situation secret. Gabe already knew and now his grandmother suspected.

Clyne sank back to the sofa, wondering what to do. He wanted her now more than ever. But pursuing her would mean going public. He wondered what kind of a hit he would take in the elections. He knew enough to know that as an Apache politician, a white, FBI agent wife would not increase his popularity. He looked at her and wondered if she might be worth it. Then she glanced at Jovanna, who was speaking to Clay about the family's cattle holdings in the tribe's communal herd.

"You better make up your mind quick," said his grandmother in a low whisper. "That girl is a mother and you don't mess around with a single mother unless you intend to marry her."

"She might not be a mother for long," said Clyne.

"She will always be that child's mother. No court in the world will change that. All you'll do is force them apart and make her choose her mother over us. But…"

Clyne looked at his grandmother but she had stopped speaking.

"What?"

"If you marry her, then Jovanna can stay with her mother."

"She's not staying on the reservation, Grandmother. Cassidy wants a transfer to Washington."

"She *wants* to stay with her daughter. And from the look she just gave you, she wants you, too. Maybe she just can't see how that would work out."

"Neither can I," he said.

In response his grandmother patted his knee and smiled.

Cassidy's phone rang, making them all jump. She glanced at the number and then took the call.

"Walker here, sir."

Her boss, Tully, Clyne knew.

"Yes?"

Clyne watched her use that index finger to plug her opposite ear as she pressed the phone to her opposite cheek. Her eyes moved restlessly as she listened. He knew the instant that it was over because she exhaled a long audible breath and her shoulders dropped a good two inches. A moment later her eyes closed for just a few seconds. When they opened they found him and she smiled.

"Yes, sir. I'll meet Agent Forrest there. Thank you."

Cassidy punched at the screen and slipped the phone away. Then she hugged her daughter.

"All clear," she said.

"What happened?" asked Gabe.

"They got him."

"Who?" asked Jovanna.

Clyne waited to see what Cassidy would do. This was the point adults sent children to their rooms or spoke in vague generalities.

"The bad man who was after me."

"You? Why?"

"His brother was a kidnapper. I caught him and...well, he died."

Jovanna cut straight to the point. "You shot him?"

Cassidy nodded, then glanced at Clyne. "I did. I had to. He was hurting someone and I had to make him stop."

"Is that person okay now?"

Her smile was sad. "No, darling. I was too late. His brother is really mad at me for hurting his brother, so he..." Here Cassidy did go vague. "He tried to hurt me. My offices figured out who it was from the fingerprints on, well..."

"A gun?"

"Something like that."

"Bullet casings," said Gabe in Apache.

Clyne nodded.

"So they chased him and arrested him and he's going to jail now."

"And you'll have to testify again?" asked her daughter.

"Yes. Likely."

"So can we go home now?" asked Jovanna.

Cassidy looked around the room at the Cosen family.

"Well, you are going home with your brothers."

"You, too?" asked Jovanna.

Cassidy's mouth went grim and Jovanna clung to her mom. Clyne glanced at his grandmother, whose brow lifted pointedly.

"You can stay in our house as long as you like," he said to Cassidy. His brothers added their consent with the simple nod of their heads.

"No," said Cassidy. "Jovanna, you remember what I told you. Six months. That's the court's order."

"But what if I get scared again?"

"Call your grandmother or any of your brothers. I trust them, doodlebug. You can, too."

Jovanna clung to her mother, who kissed the top of her head.

"You have to be strong, Jovanna. A strong Apache woman like Changing Woman."

Her daughter sniffed but then pushed herself upright and let go of her mother. That nearly broke Cassidy's heart. Her willingness to be brave and not cling like a child. She looked at Jovanna and thought she saw a glimpse of the woman she would become.

She turned to Clyne and asked him to drive her back to the station. Then she walked out the door.

Buster roused to his feet and gave a long, soulful whine of discontent.

Cassidy felt exactly the same way.

Chapter Seventeen

Cassidy buried herself in work. The interrogation of Ronnie Hare took her to Salt River for all the next day. Jovanna had not called. Clyne had not come to the hotel to fetch her. Her daughter was safe and fast becoming part of her family again. And that was as it should be.

Cassidy was no longer afraid that Jovanna would not choose her. She was now afraid that her daughter *would* choose her and by doing so, lose the family of her birth. She could see now that separating them twice was cruel and wrong. But how could she keep them together and become a part of this family?

On Saturday, Cassidy succeeded in getting her boss to agree to pay for the overtime to add additional security on Ronnie Hare. The Salt River jail was really only three holding cells in the Salt River police station. She remained at the station filling out paperwork to petition to move him to federal custody, while Luke took on the more difficult task of convincing individual members of the tribal council to vote to turn Hare over to them. They needed the consent of the Salt River tribal council to do so. Luke had spoken to the tribal chairman and, even after hearing of the charges, Luke said that he was still reluctant to relinquish custody of any of his people. If they did not, Hare would be tried here and the sentence would be very short. Luke did manage to get their chairman to at least agree to raise the matter with his fellows at the next meeting.

As for Hare himself, he was remaining tight-lipped until he knew if he would face tribal or federal court. All they could do now was wait.

"He'll spill if we have a federal case," said Luke. "He won't want to be in the same prison as Raggar."

That was the head of the American distribution ring and Cassidy agreed that turning state's witness was far better than facing Raggar's men in prison.

"We'd have no way to guarantee his safety there," she said.

"But if he plays ball we can move him to any prison, even process him under a different identity."

"He'll try for witness protection," she said.

"Not going to happen," said Luke. "We got him. I'm going to squeeze him like toothpaste until I have every last name of every last man who is involved with smuggling on the rez."

His home, she realized. His ancestral home. Cassidy filled with a deep longing for something she could only vaguely grasp. A place she belonged.

Why had she never noticed the need to be a part of a place and a community? Who was she fighting for? Americans?

Not really. She had never fought for anyone until yesterday. Yesterday she had fought for her daughter and it felt right. All this time she had been fighting against something—bad guys who broke federal law and the organization that killed Gerard. She'd never bring them all to justice. Never stop them. But the fight itself was the thing? Wasn't it?

She let the weariness weigh her down as she recognized the impossibility of the task she had set for herself. She'd never do it. Even if she made the most important case in FBI history. It wouldn't bring Gerard back.

"You all right?" asked Luke.

"Yeah. I was just thinking."

"About?"

"If I really need to go to DC to make a difference."

Luke's jaw dropped and gradually a smile replaced the stunned expression. "That's the smartest thing you've said in weeks. You staying?"

"Maybe. For a while at least."

CLYNE TOOK KAREN LITTLE HILL out on Saturday night. He usually took one of three women out, keeping it obvious to all that he was unattached. But this was two nights in a row.

Karen adjusted her shawl against the chilly air. The temperatures always dipped with the sunset, but March was susceptible to wild temperature swings.

His date had worn pants as a matter of practicality. Her necklace was Navajo and the many bangle bracelets represented most of the silversmiths in the area. She collected them the way some women collected glass figurines. Her shop at the Apache Cultural Museum showed off her knowledge of Native American Indian jewelry and pottery.

Clyne had been trying to summon up the courage to have a serious talk with Karen. Trying to gather the conviction to look her in the eyes and ask her to marry him. She'd say yes. He was certain. At least she had made her desires known to him last Christmas when he had given her a silver bangle instead of an engagement ring.

He walked her back from the restaurant to his truck, still toying with the idea of asking for her hand. He didn't have a ring, of course, except the one that had belonged to his mother and he felt loathed to give Karen that. He just felt filled with the desire to get this over with and behind him.

She beat him to her door and managed the handle without his help. Karen didn't need him. And he didn't need her. But he needed children. Ached for them.

Not just to help his tribe survive, but to fill the empty places in his heart.

"I saw a therapist yesterday," he said, once seated beside her in the dark cab.

"Why?"

"To talk about things. Things that happened while I was in the service."

"Do you think it's wise to dig up all that ancient history?"

Cassidy had encouraged him to do so, felt it was essential, in fact.

"Well, he's a medicine man and he served in Vietnam, so he knows about such things."

"I would not raise old ghosts," she said and shivered.

"Did you notice that I haven't been able to hunt since I came back home?" he asked.

"No. But it doesn't matter. We have enough guides and hunters. We need leaders. Strong role models. Which is why I was surprised to hear from Yepa that you had taken that white FBI agent to lunch."

"Gabe asked me to take her."

"You should have said no. You are the one who told me that she didn't belong here. That the federal authorities trample our rights."

"I did say that." He thought of Cassidy fighting to reach her daughter and trying to catch the man who had run messages to the cartel from the reservation. Gabe wanted that man caught and punished.

"It's bad for the people to see you with an FBI woman. It sends the wrong message."

"She raised my sister."

"I know who she is. But *you* won custody. How is Glendora managing?"

"She's fine." Clyne turned over the engine.

"She's a little old to raise a teenager."

Clyne did not dignify that with an answer.

"Your sister will need a mentor. Someone to teach her before the ceremony and mold her into the kind of woman who will make her family proud and serve her people with dignity."

"My grandmother is asking Selena Dosela."

"Selena? She's a criminal and her father was

in federal prison. I wouldn't let her anywhere near Jovanna."

"My grandmother thinks she is the right choice."

"She's wrong. It sends a bad message to the people."

Clyne set them in motion. He was not asking Karen Little Hill to be his wife. She was the perfect choice and the only emotion she raised in him was annoyance.

He knew what he felt for Cassidy was real and dangerous. But to pursue Cassidy would threaten everything he believed he was. How could he preserve their culture and their way of life if he chose a woman who knew nothing of them?

Others had married outside the community, of course. But not a tribal council member. Not one single tribal leader had married anyone other than an Apache. Clay's wife, Izzie, was Apache. Gabe's fiancé, Selena, was Apache and Kino's wife, Lea, was Apache, though she had only one clan because her mother was Mexican. But her dad was Salt River Apache.

Clyne dropped Karen at her door and gave her a kiss that left much to be desired. He couldn't help but compare the cold perfunctory touching of lips to the scorching desire stirred by just a glance in Cassidy Walker's direction. Each kiss vibrated through him like a drumbeat, building in power.

A warrior woman. A fighter.

He drew back and Karen smiled up at him. Did she feel something that he did not?

"Would you like to come in?" she asked, stroking her hand down the lapel of his overcoat.

"Ah, Karen?"

"Yes?" Her eyes were dark and bright, her mouth curled in a coy smile.

"I can't see you again."

The smile fell and her mouth dropped open.

"What are you talking about?"

"I'm seeing someone else."

Her eyes narrowed suspiciously and her words came like the hiss of a snake.

"It's that white woman. Isn't it?"

He drew a breath and then admitted it, saying it aloud.

"Yes."

"Are you crazy? She'll ruin you."

"I used to think so."

"Clyne. I know you. You're one of the most respected men in Black Mountain. And you are smarter than this."

"Goodbye, Karen. I'm sorry."

Her eyes glittered dangerously. "You will be."

Clyne left her on the stoop to her home and returned to his SUV.

Karen was going to make trouble. He knew it and he didn't care. If he was going to court Cassidy, he'd have to face this sooner or later. Many would be disappointed. But he hoped a few would see that a good woman could be Anglo as well as Apache.

He kept telling himself this as he drove to the casino hotel where Cassidy was staying. They had been strong adversaries and she was a brave woman but was she brave enough for this?

Chapter Eighteen

Clyne knocked on her hotel door and waited. He could feel her on the opposite side of the door staring at him through the peephole.

The bolt clacked, the lock turned and the door flew open.

"Jovanna?" said Cassidy.

"Fine."

She cocked her head. He saw that she was still dressed in her pants and shirt. But she wore no shoes or socks and her blazer and holster were absent. She had released her hair from the short, stiff little ponytail she usually wore so her hair fell like silk beside her face.

"What's wrong, then?"

"I needed to see you."

Cassidy still gripped the door and her opposite hand held the pistol. She motioned him in with a gesture of her head. He found her room had one king-size bed, a chair and a desk with a second chair. The only illumination came from the desk lamp and her glowing laptop that was up and open, with two files beside it on the glass surface. Near the window, her belongings were neatly folded in an open suitcase on a stand and her laptop.

"Going over some things," she said. "Can I get you something? I have pop in the mini-fridge."

"Nothing."

Cassidy sat on the bed. Clyne took the desk chair. She waited for him to speak.

"I just broke up with a woman I have been seeing."

Cassidy's pale brow lifted. Was she wondering what this had to do with her?

"I'm sorry."

"Don't be." He waved away the concern. "I told her I was seeing someone else."

Cassidy's head tilted as she thought about this.

"Are you?"

He gave his head a shake.

Cassidy's mouth dropped open as she put it together.

"Clyne...I don't think... This isn't a good idea."

"That's what Gabe said."

"This could affect my custody."

"How? She's ours for six months and then she makes a choice. Us or you. If you stay here, maybe she won't have to choose."

"Stay?" She gave her head a little shake. "So you're doing this for your sister?"

"No. For me." Clyne's head sank. He was trying every way he could think of to rationalize doing the irrational. And she was fighting him, still.

Cassidy was on her feet. "I think you should go."

"Probably." He didn't get up.

"I'm white," she said.

"No one's perfect."

She chuckled at that. Clyne stood and her eyes swept over him like a caress.

"Maybe this is just, you know, an infatuation."

He didn't think so. "Maybe."

"It's just because, well, you were over there. So was I. We understand what it was like."

"Yes. That's true. But it's more."

"I don't want this to hurt Jovanna. I don't want you thinking that sleeping with me will fix all that. I'm still her mother and I plan to win full custody."

"Even if you take her, she'll come back when she is grown. She has to."

"Why is that?"

"Because she will long to know where she comes from. Everyone needs to know that. Even if you take her for another nine years, she'll come back."

Cassidy grabbed the lapel of his topcoat and choked the fabric in her fist.

"She's my daughter."

He nodded. "Yes. She will always be that."

Her eyes filled with tears that spilled down her cheeks. He used his thumbs to brush them both aside and kept them there for a moment before threading his fingers in her fine pale hair.

He knew what he felt for Cassidy was strong and real. He also knew that marrying her would unite their families and give Jovanna her mother back. She wouldn't have to choose.

What he didn't know was if he was strong enough to face his tribe with a white woman at his side after speaking on many occasions about the need to preserve their cultural heritage.

He didn't know if he could convince Cassidy Walker to give up her transfer and stay here with them. But he wanted to try.

Clyne angled his head. Cassidy tugged at his topcoat, lifting to meet his kiss. The heat sizzled through him at the first brushing contact. He felt as if he were falling, spinning with her in his arms.

Cassidy's hands moved over his shirt, releasing buttons. He found the zipper at the side of her slacks and tugged. She let the garment fall to the ground and stepped from them. Then she sat on the edge of the bed and glanced to the empty place beside her.

He shrugged out of his topcoat and blazer and tossed them to the chair. His shirt went next. She kept her eyes on him as she released the top rivet securing his jeans. He strained against the denim fabric, showing his need in the most obvious way possible. A smile flicked over her ripe pink lips. He sat beside her and each turned to their own attire, him throwing off shoes and jeans and shirts while she slipped out of her button-up blouse. When only his boxers remained, he turned to find Cassidy standing in only a scrap of fuchsia lace panties and a lacy top with underwire lifting her small breasts so the plump flesh spilled from the shallow cup. He could see the soft pink of her nipples and the fine blue veins that crossed under the pale flesh of her breasts and belly. She was so beautiful it took away his breath.

He stood, offering his hand. She laced her fingers with his and he tugged her forward, bringing her body to his.

CASSIDY TRIED HARD not to remember the last time she had felt a man's touch. No, she pressed that down with her memories and her grief. Tonight was for the living, not the dead. And Clyne, no matter what his faults and how much they differed on every single issue, was alive and he wanted her. The attraction that roared between them created a need stronger than anything she'd ever experienced.

Tonight her need had caused her to call a truce. But it wouldn't last. What was he doing breaking up with his girl and coming here? She should have turned him around at the door, because she knew how this would end—badly.

Clyne wanted just what she wanted—to come alive, be desired, be consumed by the sweet taste and scent and feel of a perfect opposite.

But he wanted something else. He wanted her to stay and he wanted it enough to offer himself. Did he have feelings for her or was this some play to change her mind about leaving?

His strong hands lifted her until she settled on his body, a living bed of muscle and heat. Separated now by only his cotton briefs and her lacy panties, she felt the long length of him. He growled as she rocked, and lifted up to take the tip of one breast in his mouth. The dizzying sensation made her groan and arch to allow him free rein. He was not gentle. She was not submissive. No, Cassidy demanded what she wanted and took as she gave. And unfortunately for them both, their lovemaking was powerful and rare and thrilling.

Was it because it would not last?

She didn't know. But when they had finally come to rest, panting and slick with the sweat of their efforts, she closed her eyes and grieved again for this man who she feared she would never keep and for the union that marked the beginning and the end of all that could be between them.

Cassidy had a job to do here, a promotion to earn and, in six months, she was leaving Black Mountain with her daughter. Jovanna would not be coming back. She'd be certain of that.

She threw an arm over her closed eyes and purred. It was worth every bit of it, she decided.

"You okay?" he asked.

She didn't look at him. He was too handsome and seeing him in the light of one desk lamp might give her stupid ideas, like how to hold on to him.

"That was a mistake," she said.

"Are you sorry?" He rolled to his side, his fingers dancing over her stomach and making her twitch.

"Yes and no." She peered at him from under her arm. "You?"

He made a humming sound that was no answer. But his fingers continued to explore, moving from a gentle caress to purposeful stroking of her most sensitive places. Her body rose from lethargy so fast it startled her. Even with Gerard, she had never felt this kind of awareness. It wasn't fair, she thought.

"Slower, this time," he said.

She nodded. Cassidy supposed she could take some consolation in knowing that she was not the first woman and would doubtless not be the last to leave Clyne Cosen's bed wanting more.

Clyne's hand dipped lower and she moved to her back, letting him roam as he would. The man knew his way around the female form, she'd give him credit for that.

She made the mistake of looking up at him, perched on one elbow. His muscles corded at his bicep and his braid lay upon his pillow.

"Take your hair down," she said.

His brow dipped. "That some kind of white girl fantasy?" he asked, but there was still humor in his voice.

"Maybe. The men in my life were always military. Short hair. No hair. This…" she lifted his braid "…seems like a pretty good handhold."

His brows lifted and he tugged away the leather band holding his hair. He swung his legs to the floor and finger combed the three strands into one. His hair was three times as long as hers. Then he looked back at her as she rolled to her knees behind him. She reached out and stroked his black hair, finding it thick and glossy.

"Well?" he asked.

"It's nice," she said, arranging his hair over his shoulders.

"Feel free to grab hold any time," he said.

She did, moving from his hair to his shoulders and then scoring her nails over his chest. He leaned back against her as her hands moved lower and lower.

Clyne reached back, captured one knee and dragged her before him until she straddled his hips. She rose up and then down. It wasn't slow this time either, but his hair did make a very good hold.

He gripped her tight, assuring her with his touch that he would not let her fall, which gave her the freedom to move. Her daring and the trust she showed captivated. When they fell back to the mattress together she tried to just savor the retreating pleasure. But her mind kept intruding, scrambling to think of some scenario where a tribal leader would choose a white military brat who worked for the organization he mistrusted most of all, the federal government. She had a very creative mind, but Cassidy Walker could not come up with one single plausible situation where he and she could make a go of it. He should know that, too.

She closed her eyes. Clyne tucked her close. Cassidy toyed with a strand of his hair, wondering if like Samson it was the secret to his virility and strength.

Silly, she thought and allowed sleep to carry her into dreams. She expected him to leave her, steal off in the night. He did leave the bed and she tried to pretend it didn't matter. It would be easier not to face him in the morning than have to deal with what they had done. But he came back. He pulled back the still-made bed and dragged the thick comforter over them both, then he slipped against her back and tugged her close, spooning against her as he dozed.

In the morning her phone alarm stirred her from sleep. She felt the weight of Clyne's arm across her chest and groaned.

What had they done?

She silenced the alarm and rolled away. He captured her wrist before she made a clean get away.

"Cassidy, we need to talk," he said.

"I've got to get dressed."

Clyne rolled to a seat. She tried and failed not to stare at all that bare skin and muscle. His hair, still loose, fell in a tangle down his back. And then she saw it, the small white puckered place just above his left hip. The bullet must have just missed the bottom of his vest. She wanted to touch it, that tiny scar that marred his perfect flesh. But she didn't.

Instead, she turned away, took exactly what she needed from her suitcase and fled to the bathroom. By the time she emerged, showered and completely dressed, he was still there.

"Clyne, let's not do this now."

"You don't think we need to talk about this?"

"Probably. But right now I've got work."

He gave her a long look and then nodded. "So we are both going to pretend this didn't happen?"

She hesitated, shifting her weight from side to side.

"Fine," he said. "See you around, Agent Walker."

"Hey. I didn't ask you to come here."

"And you didn't ask me to leave."

"Well, now I'm asking. That can't happen again."

He snorted. "But it will. You know it will."

With that he strode out the door.

CLYNE MADE IT home to find Gabe sitting in the dining room scrolling through an Apache social media platform used by the tribe.

"Thought you'd stayed at Karen's," he said, laying the tablet on the tabletop.

"I broke up with her."

Gabe absorbed that without comment but his brows lifted high on his forehead.

"She's mad as a wet cat," said Clyne.

"Worse than when you gave her the bracelet?"

"Way worse."

Gabe rubbed his neck.

"So where'd you spend the night?" asked Gabe.

Clyne thought from the way his brother looked at him that he already knew the answer.

"Paulina? Rita?" Gabe asked, his voice holding a note of hope.

Clyne let his head drop forward. "I don't want them either."

"No?"

He met Gabe's troubled gaze.

"I want Cassidy Walker."

Gabe rocketed to his feet. "I knew it."

Clyne sighed.

"You've only known her a week."

"I met her in January when you took that shipment from the cartel."

"And you hated her on sight."

Clyne shrugged. "She's a Fed."

"I never thought I'd be asking you this but do you know what you're doing?"

"I don't think so. Rita or Paulina would be a lot easier."

"Maybe we should have a sweat tomorrow after church. Talk about this."

"Maybe."

"This isn't just a way to keep her here for Jovanna. Is it?"

"Maybe. I don't know."

Gabe's expression showed both pity and disappointment. "You really are in trouble. Never seen you like this."

Clyne poured some coffee. "Anything on that guy who tried to shoot her?"

"In custody. Charged. They're checking his prints against the partial palm print they got from the truck."

He meant the one that almost ran her down.

"You sure you can't just work her out of your system?" asked Gabe.

"How'd that work for you with Selena?"

Gabe's shoulders rose and fell. "Yeah. I get it. Well, congratulations and condolences, I guess. You are going to take some heat."

"Hypocrite. Right? Expound the need to keep our traditions and preserve our culture, and then marry a white woman."

"Does Cassidy know how you feel?"

"Nope. She didn't want to talk about it."

"Oh, man."

"Will you go with her to Washington? She's going, you know? She made a deal with Tully."

This was news to Clyne. He'd never even considered that. Leaving his home. He had told himself that after his discharge he would never leave Black Mountain again.

"Luke told me. That was the only way they could get her to come to Black Mountain. She'd come here if she got her transfer afterward."

Clyne knew Cassidy wanted a transfer. He didn't know she'd already gotten it. He felt as if Gabe had punched him.

"But the case isn't over just because they have Hare," said Clyne. "It's just starting. And it's her case."

"She doesn't want the case. She wants out."

"She won't take a transfer. Not with the ruling. Her daughter is here. So she'll stay."

Gabe gave him a pitying look. "Yeah. For six months."

Clyne felt sick.

"What about the position with the National Congress of American Indians? If you took that you'd be in Washington much of the time."

The executive director of the NCAI had asked Clyne to run for the board as vice president. He'd served as an area president for the south-west, but that did not involve much travel. VP was a different matter.

"I'm not leaving Black Mountain."

"Well, she is," said Gabe.

Chapter Nineteen

Tuesday morning Cassidy spent her second day of surveillance, watching the Wolf Posse's current place of business and kicking herself for being stupid enough to sleep with Clyne Cosen. What did he think that she'd give up her career and everything else to stay up here on this mountain? And now she was actually considering it. How stupid was that?

Glendora had allowed Jovanna to call her each day after school, but Cassidy needed something to do to keep her from going crazy or worse, calling Clyne. He said it would happen again and now she thought he was right because she could not get the man out of her head.

So here she sat on a little used road above the shabby wreck of a building used by Black Mountain's only gang. For a dead-end road, traffic in and out was brisk.

She got a call from Luke, who had been in touch with the crime lab.

"We got the report on the latents from the truck."

"The partial palm print?" she asked.

"Yeah. It's not a match for Parker."

Cassidy frowned as the implications of that rolled through her. "What do you think?"

"Not sure."

"No hits from the database?"

"None."

So the driver had no record.

"They're checking them against Donner. It's his truck so…"

"It would make sense for the prints to belong to the owner of the truck."

"Right."

Escalanti appeared before the Wolf Posse's headquarters. He did not usually leave until end of day.

"I have to go. Escalanti is moving."

"Okay." Luke disconnected.

Escalanti went to his car, removed something she could not see and returned to the house. Cassidy sighed and set aside her field glasses.

Her phone pinged, indicating a text from her daughter.

Cassidy responded to her daughter's texts throughout the afternoon and evenings but did not call, respecting the court's order in an attempt to allow her daughter to make the transition into the Cosen household. The school had her medical records. She already had a few friends. Her daughter's revelation that some of the kids called her an Anglo because she couldn't speak Apache troubled her. She did not want her daughter to enter middle school next year as an outsider. Perhaps the education Glendora insisted she begin would be valuable because it included lessons on the Apache language.

Cassidy lifted her smartphone to check Jovanna's after-school text.

taking 🐕 4 walk

Buster was in for a treat. She knew from Glendora that Jovanna took Buster on a long walk down the road and back and then played catch with him in the backyard before homework.

Cassidy texted her back.

Have fun!

KK

The reply was almost instantaneous. *KK* or *Okay*.

Cassidy recorded a new license on her pad and watched the driver, snapping a few photos.

After forty minutes or so she glanced at her silent phone and frowned. Jovanna should be back now working on homework. She lifted her phone and typed.

How was the walk?

She waited and received no reply. She furrowed her brows. Cassidy knew the cell service on the rez was spotty. But the service inside the Cosen home was good.

She stared at the blank screen, trying to decide if she should call Glendora or if she was being overprotective. Her knowledge of what happened in the world did not make her the most relaxed of parents.

She lifted her phone and dialed Jovanna. The call went to voice mail. Cassidy followed her instincts and called the Cosen home number. She got no answer so she started her engine, heading back off Wolf Canyon Road toward the town of Black Mountain.

She pulled into the Cosens' drive at the same time as Clyne arrived.

"Well, this is a surprise," he said, crossing the gravel drive to meet her.

"Where's Jovanna?"

"I don't know. Why?"

"She didn't answer my text."

Clyne did not minimize her concerns. Instead he turned toward the house. "Let's go see."

They walked through the house and the to the back where they found Glendora on the step pinning laundry to the line, the old aluminum wheel squealing with each tug.

"Where's Jovanna?" asked Cassidy.

Glendora startled. "Why, isn't she inside?"

"No," said Clyne.

Cassidy's phone rang and she blew away her relief, but when she lifted the phone it was to find the number of her boss on the screen.

"Walker," she said, scanning the wide back-yard that led up a hillside for any sign of Buster or Jovanna.

"Cassidy, you still in Wolf Canyon?"

"No. Black Mountain. My daughter's miss-ing."

"What?" Tully swore.

"Send Luke from Salt River and send a team up here now."

"You got it."

Cassidy returned the phone to her jacket.

She followed Clyne as he charged through the house and back to their vehicles. She made for her sedan.

"Do you know where she walks?"

"Yes. By the stream. This way."

Cassidy made for Clyne's SUV. He could drive. She could search.

"Let's go."

She sat in the passenger seat with her gun drawn and the window open, scanning the shoulder ahead and then the yellow grass between the road and the tree line.

Clyne also had his window open and he whistled occasionally. A high, loud commanding signal that reminded her of how a shepherd directs his dog. Then he called for Buster and then Jovanna.

She listened for a reply. Finally she heard something about a half mile from the house. It sounded like the wind but the day was flat calm.

"Stop," she cried. A moment later Cassidy saw the muddy matted fur on the animal that looked as if it had been hit by a passing vehicle. It lay in the ditch beside the road. "There." She pointed.

Clyne was out of the car at the same second as she was. Her feet hit the soft earth and sunk.

"Buster?" called Clyne.

His dog lifted his head and gave another pitiful whine. Clyne knelt beside the dog, his hand running over the matted fur.

"He's been stabbed."

Cassidy lifted her pistol to chin level and

glanced to the empty road for her missing daughter. Clyne lifted Buster up and slid him into the backseat.

"Call Gabe," said Clyne.

She did, but only after she tried Jovanna's phone unsuccessfully again. Then she called her office to initiate an Amber Alert. Finally she called Luke and Clyne drove them back to the house.

Clay and his wife, Izzie, met them in the driveway. Izzie took charge of Buster, disappearing in Clay's truck.

Kino was first on the scene and searched the property as Clyne took Clay to check the spot where they found Buster. Luke arrived and failed to get Cassidy to the safe house.

"We are going to find Jovanna," she snarled, and she left him to confer with Glendora to get a description of what exactly Jovanna was wearing. Then she joined Kino as he circled the trailer beside the house. She did not know how to read any but the most obvious tracks. She was surprised to watch him stoop and study one print after another that looked very much like all the rest to her. She followed him into the trailer and then out again. She waited where he told her as he disappeared into the woods.

The headlights told her that someone was

here and that it was getting dark. A chill gripped her. Where was her daughter?

Clay and Clyne returned as Luke arrived.

"What did you find?" asked Cassidy to Clyne.

"Buster tried to make it back to the house. He crawled a good fifty feet from where he was stabbed," said Clyne.

"Jovanna was taken by a man in an SUV or truck from the tracks. She fought him and Buster might have gotten a piece of him."

Luke broke in. "Where's the dog? There might be blood evidence on his teeth or in his mouth."

"I'll call Izzie. Ask the vet to check."

"I'm going," said Luke, rattling off the name of the vet and getting confirmation from Clay.

Kino returned, walking fast up the drive. "Someone was in that trailer."

The chill straightened Cassidy's spine and she clamped her elbows to her sides as she shook. Kino continued with his findings.

"Medium frame. Construction boots, old ones and he's pigeon-toed. He was there today. Maybe even watched Jovanna get off the bus from that window. Tracks head behind the trailer and back to the road where he got in a vehicle. We might have something by the window inside. Looks like a water bottle. I don't think it's ours."

Gabe arrived, lights flashing.

"I called everybody in. My guys and all the volunteer firefighters. They're all out looking for her."

Kino stepped aside to fill Gabe in while Cassidy called Tully with the description of Jovanna's clothing and she sent Jovanna's photo by text. Tully provided her with a GPS location on Jovanna's phone. She and Gabe set off to find it and they did, in the ditch only a mile farther up the road south, away from Black Mountain.

"Someone took her," she said.

Gabe used an evidence bag to scoop the ringing phone out of the mud and zipped it inside. Then he brought Cassidy back to the house.

Cassidy and Clyne joined the search that was now statewide. Every police officer and trooper now had Jovanna's description and if they didn't have a photo they soon would have. Plus every cell phone of anyone within a two-hundred-mile range would be receiving a special Amber Alert message. Finally, she knew all radio and television stations would broadcast the information. Even the electronic road signs would be called into service to issue the alert. And still it did not seem enough.

At 10 p.m. Clyne turned them back to the house where she spent a long night in a chair beside her silent charging cell phone. Her only consolation was that she did not wait and worry alone. She had Glendora and Clyne.

Izzie Cosen returned to report that Buster had a punctured lung and severe blood loss, but the vet was optimistic that he would survive.

"Gabe told me it was all right to tell you. There was a scrap of fabric in Buster's mouth. Olive green. Trouser material, he thinks."

Buster had at least gotten a piece of the kidnapper. Cassidy wanted the same chance. At 5 a.m. Cassidy's phone rang. She picked up.

"I've got your daughter."

"I want to speak to her."

"No."

"Who are you?"

"Ain't you figured it out yet? I'm the one that nearly run you down."

"Why?"

"My brothers is why."

Brothers. Cassidy looked at Clay, Clyne, Gabe and Kino all watching her as she took the call. Brothers who would do anything for the other.

She'd killed Brett Parker and his brother Johnny Parker had shot her in that river park. Did Brett and Johnny have another brother?

"Which Parker are you?" she asked.

"Good for you, FBI lady. I'm the youngest. No record, so I'm not in your little databases."

He'd be there now, she thought.

"What do you want?"

"I'm glad you asked."

CLYNE LISTENED AS LUKE, Cassidy and Gabe went over Parker's demands once more and final arrangements were made.

They knew the kidnapper's identity now. He was Lamar Parker, twenty-four, unemployed and a member of various survivalist organizations that might give him access to some nasty weapons.

"All we know is it's off the rez," said Cassidy. "We know what cell tower it's pinged off and it's closer to Tucson than Black Mountain."

"We can see from our satellites," said Luke. "Everything, right down to the license plate of his car to the registration on his windshield. He won't get away."

"That's not even on my list of worries," said Gabe.

Clyne felt the same way. Cassidy's life and Jovanna's life. That was what mattered. But one look at Cassidy told him she was not concerned about her own life. Only her daughter's.

"I'm worried he doesn't expect to get away," said Gabe. "He might just want to get his brother clear. Kill you and then, death by cop."

Clyne knew Lamar Parker's demands. He had

two. The release of Johnny Parker from federal prison. And then Johnny to be delivered across the border. In exchange, he would trade Jovanna Cosen for Cassidy Walker.

This couldn't be happening. He'd finally found the woman he wanted to marry and managed to get past his own issues about the expectations of others. Now he considered the possibilities that those expectations were largely his own. And now his sister's life was in danger and Cassidy was going to ride in there like the Lone Ranger minus Tonto. When everyone knew that Tonto was the only reason the Lone Ranger survived.

"I'll drive her," said Clyne.

"He'll shoot her the minute he sees you," said Gabe.

"He won't see me."

"I go alone," she said.

"He'll kill you," Clyne said.

She didn't reply, just pressed her lips tight and crossed her arms in stubborn refusal to listen to reason.

"She has to go," said Glendora. "For Jovanna."

And then he realized what his grandmother meant. Cassidy was Jovanna's mother and fully prepared to trade her life for her child's.

"My team will meet us at the reservation border. They'll be in position on every road."

Clyne turned and left the room. He walked down the hall to his bedroom, where he changed his clothes and retrieved a special case from beneath his bed. Metal case in hand, he walked to Gabe's room and reached for the key that was hanging on a nail behind the medicine wheel. Clyne gripped the key a little tighter than necessary as he faced the gun safe. Then he blew away a long breath and retrieved his rifle, scope and tripod. The ammunition box sat on the top shelf. He shoved it into his front pocket, then stooped to place each of the three pieces in the foam cradles. The fit was exact. Clyne clipped the case closed and retraced his steps. The room went silent at his return.

Gabe eyed the case he held and then met his gaze. "You remember how to shoot that thing?"

Clyne nodded. "I remember."

Chapter Twenty

Gabe's men and Cassidy's team from the FBI field office rendezvoused with a unit from the Tucson office just south of Black Mountain at the point where Cassidy was to wait for Parker's phone call.

Parker's call came in at 7:56 in the morning and, as promised, he delivered the meet location.

"I know that place. It's a bad spot," said Gabe. "First, it's a private airfield and it has a helicopter port."

Her team pulled up satellite images on the mobile operations station.

"He must know you can fly birds," said Luke.

"Second problem," Gabe said, "is that we have to cross down over a wide-open area that stretches for miles. Even at the lowest magnification, he'll see us coming if we go with you, and we don't have time to set up beforehand, and forget about a drone or aircraft." Gabe waved a hand at the blue cloudless sky. "He'll see them."

"We can put them up higher than he can see," said Tully.

"To observe," clarified Gabe.

"Yes."

Cassidy conferred with the teams and refused every suggestion that did not involve her going alone to meet Parker.

Clyne took hold of her arm to get her to focus on him.

"I'm going with you."

"He sees you, he kills your sister. I'm not taking that chance."

"He won't see me. Not from three hundred yards."

"What are you talking about?" she asked.

He pulled her toward his SUV and opened the fitted case on his front seat, showing her the foam packing in which his M24 waited beside the tripod.

Her eyes widened. She shook her head.

"You don't hunt."

"True."

"You wouldn't take my pistol."

"I know."

"So how can you expect to do this?"

"Because he has Jovanna."

She gave him a long steady look with those cool blue eyes.

"I can do it."

"We have sharpshooters," she said, her head slowing shaking a denial.

"Any of them have thirty-six confirmed kills?"

She met his gaze. "Clyne, I'm afraid."

"No. Not you."

"If he sees you…"

"Just drop your speed to twenty and I'll roll out. Then I'll set up."

She was considering it. He could tell from the amount of time she stood staring at his gear.

"You have to promise me something." Her gaze flicked to him. "If you have to choose, it will be her."

He didn't want to make that deal. This time he was shaking his head.

"Promise or I take one of them." She glanced back at her team.

He couldn't let her go with anyone else.

"All right." But he made himself a promise, too. He'd save them both. Somehow.

Cassidy went to tell her team. There was some raised voices. But the pressure of time worked in her favor. Tully aimed a finger at her. She never flinched. Finally she returned to him.

"Let's go."

Cassidy drove her sedan down the mountain with the entire army of federal agents and Gabe's men.

Clyne was glad for the tinted glass that would keep any spotter Parker might have from seeing him. There were two likely places to set up. He made his pick.

"That one."

As they drew closer he thought of all the things he needed to tell her.

"Clyne, if I don't make it back, you have to promise me to take care of her."

"You're coming back."

"She's the only one in this world who will miss me."

"I'll miss you. So come back."

She gave him a sweet sad smile.

"You took off your holster?" he asked.

Cassidy lifted her jacket, revealing an empty holster.

He hoped that Parker didn't have a set of high-powered binoculars. Clyne's mind began to sink back into the job. The average range of accuracy from three-hundred yards was three and a half inches in either direction. His was two inches.

His bullet would travel so fast that it would

reach his target in less than a quarter second of when he pulled the trigger. Too slow, Clyne decided.

"Don't shoot until Jovanna is clear," she reminded him again.

His stomach cramped in a tight little knot. But this wasn't dread. It was that mix of anticipation and the acceptance that he wanted to pull that trigger. That was the reason he had stopped. He wasn't just good at hitting a target. He found a satisfaction in a job well done. That made him a cold-blooded killer.

She drove and he held the familiar case between his legs. Inside was his M24 rifle and tripod. He had correctly guessed their location and had accordingly dressed in pale tan pants and jacket so that he would blend with the sand and soil here on the flats. In addition to this outfit, he wore elbow and knee pads. He'd had enough falls from bucking horses when he rode the rodeo circuit to know how to roll. The trick was to go with inertia and keep your arms close to your core.

"There it is," she said, spotting the hangars. There were three in this private facility. Clyne knew this facility was best known for the gliders that were towed from it and dropped so they drifted down on the updrafts on the mountains.

"Close enough. Start slowing down. I'm going on the turn. He can't tell your speed if you're coming straight at him."

She took her foot of the gas. "Clyne. Be careful."

He reached over and stroked her cheek with the knuckles of his first two fingers.

"You, too." Then he gripped the door handle and kept his eyes on the speedometer. He waited for the middle of the turn and when the needle dropped below thirty, he counted to three, threw open the door and threw himself into space.

CASSIDY WATCHED IN her rearview as Clyne tumbled over and over, gripping his case tight to his chest. So fast. Had he made it? She finished the turn and lost her line of sight to Clyne. She was alone now except for the eye in the sky and the mic that she wore and the camera/mic combo on the hood of her car grill.

Her hands were slick on the wheel. He'd be able to see her, but Clyne would watch her back as long as she stayed outside the hangar. What if Parker made her go inside? Clyne would have no shot and she would have no weapon.

Either way, she'd know soon. Three hundred yards did not take very long to cross. Had she given him enough time to get in position?

The gate was drawn open. Cassidy knew little about gliding except that it required a tow plane and the correct weather conditions. The place looked empty and she wondered if there was some season for this hobby or if it was just not economically feasible to be open seven days a week.

The still gliders looked like dinosaurs or some mechanical army waiting deployment. Most gliders only had two wheels and they sat one behind the other, so the planes tipped at an angle with one wing resting on the sandy ground. She glanced at the helicopter on the square pad of concrete. The rest of the field including the runway was graded, compact dirt.

The helicopter was gray-green and tiny. One of those Robinson R22 models with a single drooping flexible blade. The color made the resemblance to a dragonfly almost perfect. Compared to what she had flown, this was no more than a toy.

Beyond, the hangar yawned open and she just knew Parker was in there. Her earpiece came on and she heard the voice of Luke Forrest.

"They have Johnny Parker in place. He'll think he's across the river in Mexico, but he'll be about thirty miles short. Should be easy to pick him up again."

"Good," she replied. "Approaching the gate."

"Yeah. I see. Where is the little jerk?"

"No idea. Can you see Clyne?"

"Yeah. He's all set up on the hill behind you. He'll have a shot if you're not inside."

Cassidy set her jaw and drove into the airport and parked well away from the hangar and then stepped out of her vehicle and into the range of the camera on the grill.

"Parker?"

She was a sitting duck. There was just as much chance he meant to kill her while she stood here as that he intended to actually make the exchange.

"Mama!"

Cassidy turned toward the sound of her daughter's voice and saw Amanda in the seat of one of the gliders. The plexiglass cockpit had been wrapped with cable and clipped with a combination lock. Jovanna pounded a fist on the clear plastic capsule. Her face was sweat-soaked and flushed. How long had she been out in the blazing sun?

"He's got her in one of the gliders. Number Alpha Brava Two Four Six."

"Got it," said Luke in her ear.

She took a step in that direction and heard a male voice.

"Far enough."

Cassidy turned to see Lamar Parker standing

in the hangar doorway. From that position she knew Clyne did not have a shot.

"Any closer and I blow the plane."

Cassidy's heart shot right into her throat and her entire body went as cold as ice water.

"Whole backseat is filled with gas cans. Simple spark will set off the lot."

Cassidy repeated what he'd said so that Luke and the others would know of this new threat. Parker might be lying but she was not going to take that chance.

"I'm here," Cassidy said, lifting her arms and facing Lamar. That should give Clyne the direction of his target, if not the sight line he needed. "Let her out."

"Not until I hear from my brother."

"I have a phone so you can speak to him." She reached in her front pocket.

"Stop!"

She did.

"Anything but a phone comes out of your pocket and I will shoot you now."

Now. Instead of later. Parker did not plan on letting Cassidy live.

She glanced back at Jovanna, trapped in that glider. If there were gas tanks behind her, the smell of vaporizing gasoline should make her sick but she looked bright-eyed and really hot.

Cassidy lifted the mobile phone and set it at her feet. Then she backed away.

"You think I'm stupid. Bring it here."

She did think he was stupid. She'd read every scrap of paper they had on him from his failed attempt at a GED to his current job as a mechanic in a quick-lube place in Phoenix.

The phone rang and she carried it to Parker, fully expecting him to shoot her when she got within ten feet. He didn't and she tossed him the phone noticing that his weapon of choice was a shotgun. Terrible range, but you could make a mess of anything nearby without having a spectacular aim.

Parker took the call. His expression brightened.

"Johnny? You free?"

A pause.

"I did that. You in Mexico?"

Another pause.

"They give you the money? Well, that's fine. Just walk south. I'll meet you in that place by the beach in a day or two."

Cassidy narrowed her eyes. Either he could fly that bird or he thought she would fly it for him.

Parker slipped the phone in his pocket.

"Anybody else in that car?" he asked.

"Have a look."

He didn't, which was unfortunate because it would have required him to step from the protection of the hangar. Instead he disappeared from sight. She took the opportunity to walk back toward her daughter.

"Jovanna, are there gas cans behind you?"

"Yes."

Her heart gave a flutter and then squeezed with such an ache she had to press a hand over it.

"I'll get you out."

"Be careful. He's mean. Mama, he killed Buster."

"Buster is okay. He's at the vet."

And that bit of news was the straw that made her brave little girl begin to cry.

Parker reemerged from the hangar driving a postal truck that had the driver seat situated on the opposite side. He now wore a helmet and something that looked like body armor. He made for the helicopter pad.

"Deals a deal," he yelled. "Go on and let her out."

Cassidy wondered if he meant to blow her and Jovanna to pieces and then fly himself off. But she still ran to the glider. She was now separated from Jovanna by only a thin piece of plastic and the cable that held the glider like a steel boa constrictor.

"Combination!" Cassidy shouted.

Parker had reached them now but he provided the numbers and Cassidy spun the dial back and forth until the mechanism released. She threw the lock and cable over the top of the glider and then hauled it from below, repeating the action again and again until the cable finally dropped to the ground.

"Mama?" Jovanna said and pointed.

A glance behind her told her two things: Parker had the shotgun aimed at her back and Clyne still had no shot. She knew her body armor would stop most of the birdshot, but not any that hit her head. But she could at least protect Jovanna from the blast.

"Pull the toggles up front," she said.

Her daughter did and the capsule flipped open like a clear burger container. No smell of gas. She glanced to the small space surrounding the single seat, spotting gallon jugs that looked like water. She didn't know what was in there and didn't want to know.

Cassidy hugged her daughter tight and dragged her clear, keeping her back to Parker.

"Let her go," he ordered.

She did, dropping her on the far side of the glider as she whispered to Jovanna.

"When you can, run for the gate and keep running. Clyne is out there waiting for you."

"What about you?" she asked.

"I'll follow." She hoped that would be the case.

Cassidy released her child, who ducked behind the glider. Parker didn't seem to notice or care.

"Get in," he ordered.

She did, knowing that when he turned the truck, Clyne would have the shot. But Parker put it in Reverse.

"So what's the plan?" she asked.

"You fly me out of here, is what."

"I can't fly that."

"You can. You said you were a pilot in the Middle East. I heard you."

So he had been in court that day.

"My daughter goes free. You promised."

"She is free."

"You expect her to walk back to Tucson?"

"You think I don't know they're out there? I ain't that stupid."

If that were true he wouldn't be dressed in a combination of body armor and hockey gear driving a mail truck, she thought.

"Fine. Let's go."

He stopped the truck as if he knew where the sharpshooter might be and managed to get into the chopper without making himself a target.

Cassidy took her seat and started flipping switches. "So what happens when we reach Mexico?"

Parker gave her a chilling look. "You stop breathing and I meet my brother."

"Not much incentive for me."

"Or," said Parker, "I run your daughter down with the mail truck and shoot you here and now."

Cassidy started the engine and the damned prop rotated. She considered tipping the bird and dropping Parker to the ground, but he clipped himself in tight before she was off the ground. And then it came to her and she knew exactly what she would do.

Chapter Twenty-One

"Come on, Cassidy," Clyne whispered. "Give me the shot." The cheek piece touched his face like an old friend. He had the sights adjusted and the target, well that was the trouble. Damn little weasel wouldn't pop his head out of the burrow. Clyne cursed under his breath.

Jovanna huddled behind the glider and Cassidy was in the chopper preparing to lift off. But he could tell by the slight inclining of her head that she'd heard him. He waited, knowing this was a shot he could not miss.

The chopper lifted a foot off the ground. She swung it around, hovering so that the large clear plastic windshield gave him a perfect view of them seated side by side. He aimed and squeezed the trigger.

Parker jerked in his restraints and sagged. What was left of his head sagged forward. Cassidy set down the chopper and slipped to the ground, running bent over and low to keep clear of the whirling blades. She ran to her daughter, shouting her name.

"Jovanna! Jovanna!"

They met and clasped each other, sinking to their knees in the dust and he wondered how he had ever thought to pull them apart.

Gabe had been right and he had been a fool. But one of the good things about mistakes was that you could often make amends. Above him one of the FBI choppers roared across the clear blue sky toward Cassidy and Jovanna.

Clyne stood and dusted the sand from his shirt. Then he disassembled his scope and tripod from the rifle and stowed them neatly away. For the last time, he hoped.

Number thirty-seven, he thought. But somehow he knew that this kill would not haunt his dreams.

Clyne started walking toward Cassidy. He had an important question for her and for Jovanna.

CASSIDY SAW CLYNE walking along with his rifle case looking like a soldier coming home. She left Jovanna with Luke and ran the last thirty feet that separated them, throwing her arms wide and leaping at him. He dropped his case and caught her easily, whirling her around and round until settling her against him in a bear hug of an embrace. Kisses followed, raining down on her eyelids and cheek and finally finding her mouth.

She drew back, her hands still locked behind his neck and his clamped behind her lower back. She didn't care that every single member of her field office was there or that her daughter was seeing her kissing her brother. None of that mattered. Just this and her daughter's safety. It was more than enough.

"You did it!" she said.

"Thanks for giving me a target."

"We make a good team."

He nodded. "But I think you are blowing your transfer." He inclined his head toward her boss, who regarded her with hands on hips.

"I'm not accepting a transfer," she said.

"No?"

"Nope," she said and kissed him again.

Clyne drew back as Jovanna made a tentative approach. Clyne scooped her up in his arms, making her squeal with delight. Then he settled her on his hip and touched his head to hers, speaking in Apache.

"What did you say?" she asked.

"I said that you need to learn Apache!"

Jovanna's brow furrowed.

"And I thanked the one above for your return."

She grinned. "So…you and my mom."

"Yeah. What do you think?" he asked.

Cassidy held her breath and her daughter's gaze went from Clyne to her and then back to her eldest brother.

"I'm good with it."

Cassidy blew out a breath and her shoulders sagged a bit. Clyne set Jovanna down. But she kept a hold of him and reached for her mother. The three embraced and Cassidy began to cry.

"It's okay now, Mom."

It was and that was precisely why she was weeping.

The Bureau took them by helicopter back to Black Mountain, where they were greeted by Glendora, Clay, Izzie and Kino's wife, Lea. Gabe and Kino were driving back and would be arriving soon. Johnny Parker had been retrieved and had already been returned to federal custody to await trial.

"Catalina's for lunch," said Clay after his grandmother had finished fussing and weeping over the return of her granddaughter.

Cassidy set off with them, walking the short distance from tribal headquarters to Catalina's restaurant but slowed to take another call. She listened, finger in opposite ear, nodding and then said a quick thank-you. She tucked away the phone.

"That was Luke. He heard from Red Hawk, the police chief on Salt River. The council met last night and voted to turn Hare over to federal custody."

Clyne absorbed that news. She knew it was a difficult thing for a tribe to release one of their own.

"We will have a much better chance of getting his cooperation now," she offered.

"We? So you're staying?" he asked.

"It's my case."

He smiled.

"Yes. I know," said Clyne.

Cassidy glanced toward his family, who were just disappearing into the restaurant. Clyne did not move except to shove both hands in his coat pockets and sway from side to side.

Cassidy eyed him suspiciously. "What's wrong?"

"Why does something have to be wrong?"

"Because I know you and you're nervous." She pointed at his sweating upper lip.

He wiped it with his sleeve and tried for a calming breath. "I went to see someone, as you recommended."

"A therapist?"

He nodded. "And he is also a medicine man. I'm going to go twice a week and try to work out my issues."

"That's great. I'm proud of you."

"You were the one who made me realize I had issues. Maybe in time the nightmares will go away."

"Mine have." She made a face. "Mostly."

"You said down there that you aren't taking the transfer. What did you mean?"

"Just that. Jovanna is happy here, so I'm staying."

"Even after she makes her choice?"

"I don't think she should have to choose."

He felt the knot in his stomach ease. "Neither do I."

"That's a switch," she said, her smile bright as sunlight on Black Mountain.

"I've made a lot of switches lately. I want you here with us. Not just for weekends or when Jovanna has a nightmare."

She cocked her head and her smile faded. He was making an ass of himself. Babbling. He was usually so composed, but Cassidy just stripped him bare.

"What do you have in mind? Joint custody?"

"Not exactly. I want to marry you, Cassidy."

He'd succeeded in shocking her judging by the way her mouth dropped open as if it was on a hinge. She snapped it shut and her pale brows lifted on her forehead.

"I'm not an Apache woman."

He chuckled. "Yes. I noticed."

"But what about your position on the tribal council and in the community?"

"Cassidy, my heart has to come before my position and my ambitions. And you are my heart."

"Your what? Clyne, I don't understand." She glanced in the direction his family had gone. "What about your brothers? Your tribe? What will they think?"

"Cassidy, I still care about their opinions, but they come second now to my own. I know what I want. The only question left is what do you want?"

She still resisted, drawing away. His heart squeezed in his chest as the seconds slowed to a stop.

Finally she spoke. "Are you doing this for Jovanna? So she won't lose me?"

"Yes."

Cassidy's face fell.

"And no. I realize it will be best for Jovanna. I know I can be both brother and father to her. Long ago, when my mother left my dad, I supported this family. I can do that again. But I asked for you to marry me because I love you."

Tears rose, filling her lower lids and making her blue eyes seem to swim.

He released her hand and then unclasped the medicine bundle from his neck. It took only a moment to fish the ring from the mix of sacred objects he carried with him. His mother's ring, already purified and blessed by the smoke of sage and cedar. He had polished the white gold band and cleaned the central diamond flanked by two additional smaller stones. Then he took a page from the white culture and dropped to his knees right there behind tribal headquarters.

"Cassidy, will you be my wife?"

She reached for the ring he offered.

"It was my mother's. I always planned to give it to my wife, but you can choose another if you like."

She hesitated and then offered her left hand. He slipped the ring over her left index finger. She righted it with her thumb and then extended her finger for him to admire. He kissed the back of her hand.

"You're blowing my cover," she whispered.

"Is that a yes?" he said.

"Yes."

Cassidy lunged as he rose and they held each other as their mouths joined for a kiss filled with possession and promise.

She now held the heart of the man that made her want to put down roots. Instead of saving the world, Cassidy now wanted only to save this small corner of it. She could help him protect this family, his people and this place. His family would become her family, the one she had always longed for. Another blessing. A place, a purpose, a home, a family and a husband.

He stroked her cheek, smiling down at her.

"You make me want to sing."

"And play the flute?" she asked.

He laughed. "Yes. I will play it for you."

"I'm so lucky to have found you," she said, resting her cheek on his chest. "All of you."

"Do you still want to go to Washington?" he asked. "Because I would go with you if it makes you happy."

"You would do that?"

"If it is what you want."

"Maybe when Jovanna is a little older, for high school. We could go for a few years, then come back."

"I could see about a job in DC. I have some contacts there."

She raised her eyebrows. "Really?"

He shrugged. "Sure. Lobbyist, activists, even BIA has Native Americans on salary."

"I didn't know that."

He smiled.

"Well, right now I think Jovanna needs her family and community the most. She needs Black Mountain."

"Bear born of Eagle," said Clyne.

She glanced toward the restaurant.

"Look." She pointed.

There was her daughter in the center of the picture window, standing between her grandmother and brother Clay. Beside them, his brother's wives crowded close. All of them were looking at them and cheering. She met the gaze of Selena Dosela, who stood beside Glendora. Her daughter's mentor, she realized and smiled.

Clyne tucked her close to his side and stood tall. "You ever been to an Apache wedding?" he asked.

"Ours will be my first," she said.

He laughed and set them in motion toward their family.

Epilogue

Four months later

Cassidy stood beside her husband in the circle of onlookers as her daughter prepared for the third most important day of the four-day ceremony. Jovanna had successfully completed ceremonies and rites with her mentor and the medicine man. On Thursday the men had made the wikiup for Jovanna where she received instruction. That night there was dancing and songs. The next day Jovanna was ritually molded by Selena into a new woman and then she danced for over six hours. She had danced and sang thirty-two songs. Once the ceremonies began, her daughter could not touch water and so was fed through a reed by her mentor. Saturday morning, Jovanna greeted the sun, still dancing with both Selena and Clay's wife, Izzie, at her side. Lea, now a new mother with a three-month-old baby, had joined them on and off but had been there at sunrise.

Then, after only a few hours rest, Jovanna was preparing to dance for the last time. Glendora had made her ready for the blessing. Soon she would transform to Changing Woman to bring good health and fortune to the people assembled.

Earlier Cassidy had stood in the juniper wikiup with her new husband, Clyne, and their immediate family as the medicine man presented her daughter with the crooked oak cane that would give her strength for the rigorous dancing to come. Bright ribbons fluttered in blue, yellow, black and white from the wooden staff. Clyne had told her that these colors represented the four directions.

Jovanna still wore the colorful camp dress of the first and second day when she had carried the food she had prepared to the sweat lodge where the medicine man and her brothers prepared the sacred objects for this rite.

Cassidy's husband, Clyne, stood beside her, whispering words to explain the Apache prayers. She was beside herself with curiosity to hear the name the medicine man would give her daughter. But that would come tonight after the songs were sung.

Her sisters-in-law had shared their Apache

names. Gabe's fiancé, Selena, was Sunflower Woman. Clay's wife, Isabella, was Medicine Root Woman. Kino's wife, Lea, was Morning Star Woman.

This evening Jovanna's dance would be the most sacred as she and the five Crown Dancers joined to transform her into the physical embodiment of Changing Woman.

The medicine man left them and Cassidy went with the women to help Jovanna dress for her final dance. They returned to the wikiup where Selena stripped Jovanna out of her camp dress. Now her grandmother slipped the elaborately decorated white leather buckskin over her granddaughter's head. The fringe, representing the rays of the sun, fluttered as the top piece settled into place. An eagle feather was tied to her hair by Selena, Jovanna's mentor. Next Glendora tied the symbol of Changing Woman to a lock of Jovanna's hair so that the tear-shaped abalone shell sat centered on her forehead.

Her daughter was transformed before her eyes, standing proud and straight as prayers were spoken and instructions given.

Jovanna moved to stand in the opening of the wikiup. The medicine man sprinkled yellow bee pollen over Jovanna's dark head, the fine powder trickling down as bright as sunlight on dark water. He smudged more pollen on her cheeks.

Then they move from the domed hut of juniper and out to greet the guests, who cheered. Selena and Glendora remained in place. This was a dance that Jovanna would perform with only the Ga'an, the crown dancers.

The drums began and Jovanna bounced, bending both knees in time to each beat matching the drummers' pounding rhythm with a strike of her sacred cane. Her brothers disappeared, going, Cassidy knew, to change into the Ga'an, the mountain spirits who would paint Jovanna's skin white and make her Changing Woman.

The drum sounded. Jovanna bobbed, dipping over seven hundred times by Cassidy's count for just one dance. Where did she find the strength?

The jangling of thousands of sleigh bells announced the appearance of the Crown Dancers. Cassidy turned to see them approach. Each of the four Cosen brothers now wore a black hood that completely covered their heads. They also wore moccasins and leather aprons. Strands of bells circled their calves and waists. Their torsos were now painted entirely in white, a mixture of corn flour and clay that Jovanna had ground with her own hands for this purpose. In addition there were symbols painted on their chests and backs by the medicine man. Each man carried a white wooden sword and Cassidy noted that each was different, as were their wooden crowns. The fifth dancer looked similar to the others but for the white mask and the different headdress. Also his body had been painted black. This was Luke, she knew, who was for this dance the Sacred Clown.

The crowns of the dancers did not resemble what she thought of as a crown except that they fit on their heads. They rose high and were constructed of painted wooden frames. She thought they looked like wooden fencing and were shaped like an open fan. She recognized something that resembled a moon on the top of one and something similar to a snowflake on another. One was a medicine wheel, or was it a hoop? She wasn't certain.

Jovanna greeted their arrival by joining them as they circled. The dance went on and on, with all the players moving in coordination to the chanted prayer and the beating drum.

She knew they were spirits now, but she recognized the men beneath. Gabe was the most heavily muscled and his chest held the pattern of a wolf print, which she found appropriate for a police chief. Kino, the slimmest, had a symbol of what looked like two snakes on his chest. Clay, the tallest, had a series of large black spots on his chest. Cassidy finally stared at Clyne. Tall and handsome, his crown bobbed as he lifted his wooden sword. The others followed. What was the triangle on his chest symbolizing? It puzzled her and then she knew because of its flat top. Not a triangle. Black Mountain, the place closest to his heart, the land he had returned to in order to be at peace.

The men now surrounded Jovanna. The bowl of paste made from clay and cornmeal was given to Jovanna and she held it in two open hands. Clyne used a grass brush to paint his sister white. Down over her face. Across the beautiful leather dress, into her long loose hair went the paint, covering the dusting of bee pollen that had been sprinkled on her head and smudged on her cheeks, until even Cassidy had to admit, she could not recognize her child. She had transformed into a strange mysterious female—Changing Woman. White Painted Woman. White Shell Woman. Mother to all the Apache People. A sacred goddess.

Cassidy had a chill as she watched her move about the ring of spectators who stood in reverence at her passing.

Jovanna would not touch her face and no one would touch her now as the group made their way about the circle. Clyne used the brush of reeds to fling white paint from the bowl held by Changing Woman onto the assemblage. The

Apache believed that her daughter now had the power to heal, bring rain and cure illness. Many in the crowd opened their hands to receive the blessings of Changing Woman as she passed.

Her daughter, who had come to her as a small girl, had at this moment become a woman.

Cassidy found herself bobbing in time, supporting her daughter as did they all. Encouraging her to have strength to endure the rigors of life.

Jovanna was surrounded by a circle of her family, clans and tribe. Only her grandmother, Diane, was absent, having decided to move back east to her family after Cassidy and Clyne's May wedding on Black Mountain.

Jovanna moved in time with the beat as she danced about the inner circle giving her blessing to the gathering and received their blessings in return for fertility, happiness, health and long life.

After the dancers had circled they danced again. But none would touch Changing Woman until all the sacred songs and dances were done. She did not know where her daughter found the strength. Perhaps from the mountain itself. But she went on and on as the sun set.

As her daughter passed again, the white paint flew from the bundled grass brush. Flecks of white splattered on Cassidy, Glendora and the wiggling baby Tao, who gurgled in his great-grandmother's arms, the blessings falling upon them like rain.

A runner entered the ring, lighting the central bond fire.

The Crown Dancers, bobbed, their bells jangling, now dark silhouettes against the fire's light. As they chanted and spun, the orange flames illuminated their painted bodies until Cassidy thought they did seem more spirit than man.

Suddenly and with no warning Cassidy could recognize the drums ceased. Silence echoed.

It was done. The Ga'an spirits disappeared from the ring, returning to the mountain.

The medicine man spoke, giving blessings to all who supported this woman as she danced for them. At last he gave Jovanna her name. First he said the names of her family and Cassidy heard her name uttered with the Cosens'.

As he spoke Glendora translated.

"He says, she is Bear from her father and Eagle from her mother. He says, this woman has returned to the place of her birth after vanishing like the moon above."

Glendora listened and smiled, nodding her approval of the name.

"Your daughter has earned the name Mountain Moon Woman because she is strong as the mountain and, like the moon who disappears, she always comes back."

Clyne appeared beside her, slipping his arm about his wife's waist.

"That was wonderful," Cassidy said.

Jovanna came toward them. Cassidy clasped her hands before her to keep from reaching out.

"It's okay," said Glendora. "It's over. You can touch her now."

Cassidy drew her arms around her daughter, who sagged in weariness against her. Clyne's arms encircled them both.

"Welcome home, Mountain Moon Woman," said Cassidy and kissed Jovanna's painted forehead. Then she released her daughter so she could accept congratulations from others.

Clyne dropped a kiss on Cassidy's lips. He tasted of chalk and smelled of sweat and leather. She wondered if now would be a good time to tell him that he was soon going to become a father to not just Jovanna, but the new life kicking inside her.

"I think some of that bee pollen got on me," she said.

He smiled and nodded. She swept her hand down over the slight swelling of her stomach.

Clyne's eyes went wide as understanding

dawned and he gave a cry of pure joy and elation as he swept her up in his arms.

He set her down before her and spoke in Apache.

"What did you say?" she asked.

"I said that I love you, Cassidy Walker Cosen, now and forever."

* * * * *